Skies
of
Navarys

Also by J.M. Ney-Grimm

Resonant Bronze

Rainbow's Lodestone

Star-drake

Sarvet's Wanderyar

Crossing the Naiad

Livli's Gift

The Troll's Belt

Perilous Chance

Troll-magic

Skies
of
Navarys

A Lodestone Tale

by J.M. Ney-Grimm

Wild
Unicorn

ISBN-13: 978-0615880327
ISBN-10: 0615880320

Designed by JMNG

Cover art by Luca Oleastri / Dreamstime.com

For Dad

Skies
of
Navarys

*T*he tale is usually told with the great Palujon Clisto as rogue and thief, and the legendary Zandro Mytris as hero and savior. But one mother of ancient Navarys knows the truth.

She was there on the fabulous airship *Subindo*, the only one of the fleet to ride untouched through the storm.

Liliyah clutched the back of the divan where she knelt, bounced once, and pressed her face to the slanted window pane of the airship. The glass felt cool against her nose tip.

"Look! Look!" she exclaimed. "It's Eirene! Going to the park."

"How can you tell?" Mago's shoulder nudged hers as he peered downward. "We're way too high to tell who's who."

"She always goes now. Besides, I just know. It *is* her." Why did Mago have to doubt everything? He'd been nicer when they were younger. Now it was always "are you sure?" and "why do you think that?" and never just taking her say so. Liliyah gritted her teeth, then refocused on the panorama below.

This was her first time up in the *Subindo,* and seeing home from the air was amazing. The ocean surged vast and blue-gray from horizon to horizon. The island of Navarys, stretching away under the noon sun, showed so many textures of green: dark of pine, bright of meadow, and cool of orchard. And the city tumbled down the western slopes of Mount Sohlon like an infant's set of playing blocks: pierced cubes of colored marble and stucco roofed by verdigris copper or olive tile. *Mother should see this!* She'd be searching through her reticule for paper and stylus the instant the rooftop canvas revealed itself to her, eager to sketch designs for this new dimension.

Liliyah watched her nurse, tiny as an ant at this height, pause in their courtyard by the vivid purple patch – the tubs of balloon flowers – before passing under the gate to the street.

"That *is* my house," Liliyah insisted.

"Yeah. I guess. But how do you know it isn't one of the maids? Or a footman? Or even your mother?" Mago clung to his skepticism.

"'Cause they're bony thin, not plump like Eirene." Liliyah could be stubborn too. She fingered the decorative bronze catch of the window casement. The metal was cool, like the glass, and its scrolling curves soothed her irritation. Mago puffed out a breath of exasperation, and Liliyah shifted her gaze to his face. His brows contracted slightly over his hazel eyes, and his lips, more usually curved in the hint of a smile, had thinned. "You always jump to conclusions!" he burst out. "With never a smidge of evidence! Why are you always so irrational?"

"I'm not irrational! And I do have evidence! My house, a round figure wearing Eirene's amber head scarf, enjoying the flowers, and leaving at her usual time. How can you be so slow and stupid?" Liliyah felt her own eyes widening in a glare and her chin jutting. "Don't you understand that every last detail needn't be pinned down and labeled in order for you to know something? What d'you have to have? A view through a spyglass with Eirene smack in the middle of the lens?"

"Yes! Exactly!" Mago turned abruptly to sit a small distance away from her on the divan they shared. "Details matter! Precision matters! Fudging the facts can be dangerous."

Liliyah sat back on her calves, her back to the low table of finger foods and the gondola aisle beyond it, her attention fully on her friend. What in the world did he mean? "How could mistaking, oh, Dama Mytris" – his mother – "for Eirene possibly be dangerous?" Her astonishment was cooling her aggravation.

Mago vented an embarrassed laugh. He was calming too. "Well, it couldn't be Mama, of course." His mother sat gossiping with her friend at the far end of the gondola, nibbling on the chilled grapes, and sipping iced coffee. She'd changed seats soon after exchanging stiff greetings with the dark-haired man who took the divan next to hers. "But such a mistake could be risky." Mago straightened his spine."

"How?" Liliyah felt more and more puzzled. Social discomfort, yes. Risk? No. She reached for a grape from the platter behind her, met the bowl of salted nuts instead, and lifted a pecan to her lips. Its barky scent brought her family's front parlor before her mind's eye, a comfortable space where a bowl of in-the-shell nuts always graced the central table.

"What if you mistook an enemy for a friend? What if that weren't Eirene? What if it were someone who hated you putting an *energea* stone in your fountain to make you sick?"

Liliyah shivered and pulled her pelisse more snugly around her shoulders. Inside the airship's gondola was warm, stuffy even. But a casement several panes down from the one she'd been looking through was open, and the breeze from it, chilly. "No one hates me," she asserted. "And *energea* stones are safe. My papa makes sure they're safe." He did, too. Before Liliyah was born, her father and a friend of his had founded a commission to test the *energea* stones and determine safe levels for their powers.

The limited ones used by small crafters – cheesemakers, weavers, potters – to speed and mechanize parts of their work were unlikely to cause harm. But the newer and larger stones being developed for mining and smelting and earth-moving had worried Daymo Lykos, and he'd taken action. Rightly, as it turned out. The old, traditional *energea* stones drew energy from the things and people near them, but in such minute amounts as to be imperceptible. The new stones drew much, much more; sometimes too much. Daymo Lykos' commission had intervened before anyone was hurt. And the Navarean monarch had not only awarded Liliyah's father the Olivine Guerdon in honor of his work, but had created a royal corps that assessed and certified every stone in their island kingdom every year.

"*Energea* stones are safer than they've ever been," Liliyah insisted.

"Except the ones that go untested." Did Mago sound glum?

Liliyah was tired of being patient with him. "There are no untested stones! My father sees to that!" she snapped.

"Oh, yes, there are."

"Do you just enjoy being sad and mad or something? 'Cause I don't! What's wrong with you, Mago?"

"*I* prefer being accurate over illusory happiness" – an unbearably superior tone – "as you clearly don't, Demoselle Lykos. Fine! Be glad and ignorant. I don't care. You're only a baby anyway. With a nurse."

Speechless, Liliyah jerked to her feet. "You, you – crass and loutish boor!"

"Better than a silly goose who wouldn't know logic if it crawled up her nose!" Mago's chin lifted.

Liliyah's chin jutted, but she bit her tongue. *I won't say it. Won't.*

The smooth voice of the man disdained by Dama Mytris interrupted their quarrel. "I think you'd both best aim for a do over." He sounded amused and sympathetic together. "Roll back to when the steward brought refreshments," he advised.

Mago flushed and looked at the carpeting.

Liliyah surveyed the stranger. Unlike her papa, no gray in his hair, but the same faint smile lines at his mouth and a calm intentness behind his gaze. Who was he? Did she know him?

"Palujon Clisto, demoselle," he introduced himself.

Oh! She didn't know him, but she knew *of* him. Daymo Clisto was the most gifted aeromancer on the island, responsible for adjusting the weather along the routes followed by the Navarean merchant fleet. Half the wealth of Navarys depended on his skill.

"Liliyah Lykos," she returned, "and Mago Mytris."

"We've met," muttered Mago. Then, fixedly: "My apologies, Daymo Clisto." He lifted his eyes. Was that desperation in their depths? "But you know I'm right, sir, don't you?"

"Partially." The aeromancer smiled. "Your friend here looks pretty sharp to me." He nodded at Liliyah. "Nothing like a silly goose or an enemy to logic." He winked.

Mago's flush deepened. He turned to Liliyah. "I . . . didn't really mean that, Lili. I – I'm worried, that's all. About someone else who's ignoring . . . possibilities."

Palujon poured three glasses from a carafe of peach juice and raised his in a toast. "To logic, to intuition, to friendship!"

Vivid sweetness from her sip filled Liliyah's mouth. Yum.

"You were once my father's friend," Mago blurted after swallowing.

"I was," Palujon answered. "We served as apprentices under the royal engineer back in the day. Since then our ways have lain apart."

"But more so now," Mago challenged him.

"Yes."

What was Mago wanting? Liliyah studied him. He'd grown away from her these last two years, caught up with lessons and the concerns of the boys' school where he enrolled. His shoulders had broadened, and a light fuzz glimmered on his upper lip. He'd changed. Yet he was the same, too: mostly genial, sociable, and kind. Today's tension was not usual. Anxiety, belligerence, and pleading chased across his expression.

Palujon continued, "Daymo Mytris and I differ on the matter of his latest research, but this is not the place for discussion about it. And you, as his son, are not the person for me to discuss it with."

"I think you are right about my father. I *fear* you are."

Liliyah chewed her lip. Zandro Mytris engineered *energea* stones, the big ones. Her papa often said they were the most efficient for their size of any on the island. And the safest, drawing the least energy for the most output. Zandro and Papa had been friends for decades. Their families met often to dine or ride or attend the opera together. That was why Dama Mytris had invited her on this pleasure expedition in the air. Liliyah peeked out the window bank again. The airship had moved beyond the city and its harbor, hovering over the grand circus where the chariot races were run. She glanced back to where Mago's mother laughed with her friend, oblivious to her son.

Had Papa displayed a coolness toward Daymo Mytris lately?

"Talk with your father," Palujon suggested, "or a family friend. You must know that you should not talk with me, and I cannot talk with you about him."

Mago's lips compressed. "Yes, I know. But – oh, sir, can't you *do* something?"

Palujon shook his head. Not a refusal to act, Liliyah guessed, just a refusal to talk.

What was Daymo Mytris up to? Would Mago tell her? *I'll make him tell*, she decided. *The next time Mama drags me to walk in the park with her when she meets Dama Mytris.*

The rest of the afternoon on the *Subindo* passed pleasantly enough. The airship toured all the notable landmarks – the lighthouse marking the Gorgon's Rocks, the cliff face carved in the likeness of Queen Cybele, the Minotaur's Gorge, and the rest – and Mago relapsed into his more relaxed self as Daymo Clisto guided the conversation into social channels. Had Mago tasted the apricot pastries at the new bakery on Strato Street? What did Liliyah think of the new style for sandals, with the three straps at the ankle? Had either of them seen the new star discovered by the royal astronomers?

The only awkward moment came as they approached the air terminal. The *Subindo* was the largest of the fleet of airships, able to accommodate three gangways rather than the usual one, and it often docked at the main loggia instead of one of the four outlying mooring towers. Liliyah followed Mago and Palujon to the foremost span to disembark. They were just marveling over the frescoed vault of the gallery visible beyond the loggia – an image of Evaia, goddess of the sea, dancing with her sister, Caecia, goddess of the winds – when Dama Mytris joined them, preceded by a drift of her lilac perfume. Liliyah sneezed.

"Bless you, child." Her tone was indulgent until she acknowledged Palujon. She must have noticed that her son and his guest enjoyed the aeromancer's company for the majority of the voyage, but her demeanor belied it. "Surely the center gangway or that aft would be more appropriate?" She sniffed, tilted her head back, and looked down her nose.

Palujon quirked his left eyebrow. "My tenor displeases you, Dama?" His tone conveyed irony.

"Your mere presence suffices," she snapped.

Mago interposed uneasily, "Daymo Clisto has been most kind all afternoon, Mama."

"Let him dispense children's entertainment to others than Zandro Mytris' progeny then." His mother sniffed again, and her dark eyes flashed. "You dare too much, Daymo!"

"Indeed, you are correct, Dama. I'll relieve you of my daring."

Liliyah wrinkled her forehead. Was he apologizing for social effrontery or insulting Dama Mytris for her dislike of boldness?

Palujon touched Liliyah's shoulder. "'Twas a pleasure to meet you, demoselle. Your father and I" – was there a touch of emphasis on your? – "have grown busy in our separate professions, but we remain friends. I hope to encounter you again." Then he was gone, stepping from the gangway's heel and vanishing in the crowd.

Liliyah never got her opportunity to grill Mago about his father.

That evening she accompanied her parents to the Grand Exhibition Hall. The Corps of Royal Engineers were holding a gala reception at the unveiling of their proposal for a rail line to connect the copper mines to the shipyards. The arcade just inside the quadruple portals was jammed with notable guests. Dama Jeno, one of Mama's cronies, swept out of the crush to greet them. "Persis, my dear! Daymo Lykos! It's just too amazing! My husband declares it will ruin our green countryside, but I think the device is clever. Have you seen it?"

Liliyah's papa bowed. Her mama laughed, a ripple of pleasant sound. "How should I? We've just arrived, Zephyra. Where is the miniature?"

"Just beyond the columns." Dama Jeno waved a careless hand. "But you must meet Daymo Eryx first. He's longing to compare notes with you and your husband. And you'd best doff your wraps." She fluttered her fan, puffing the scent of roses through the warm air with its silver-encrusted panels.

Liliyah had already shrugged out of her pelisse. The thin silk of her frock, too light for the chill of the night air, was welcome in this overheated gathering space. Its pale turquoise folds felt cool and smooth against her body. She craned her neck, trying to see around Dama Jeno to where the "clever device" stood on display, but the crowd was too dense.

They edged past a matron displaying purple feathers in her headdress and flashing diamonds around her throat, nibbling dainties of sweet almond paste, and talking nonstop with an excited acquaintance. They were not the only pair so animated, rather than fashionably bored. A buzz of enthusiasm pervaded the space. Liliyah's parents paused again for more meeting and greeting. Their progress remained slow, and Dama Jeno eventually peeled away before they reached the man she intended to present to them.

Daymo Eryx proved to be one of the civil engineers who devised the engine that would travel on the new railway. "With just a slight change in the gearing ratios, we can make it work with the old *energea* stones," he was declaring seriously to Liliyah's papa. "The lever to disengage the flywheel is probably a good idea even when the power source is not continuously supplying power the way these newfangled lodestones do."

Daymo Lykos nodded genially. "I reviewed your schema a few days ago and was pleased to note your variants. Truly excellent, proactive work, Daymo. I wish all inventors would pursue a branching strategy."

The engineer's eyes lit with enthusiasm. "Are you a fellow devotee of systematic thought?"

"A mere smatterer, I'm afraid." Papa's voice sounded regretful. "But the systems approach yields multiple solutions before they are needed, which prevents incidents like the Heremias disaster. A narrow, focused approach may be efficient, but prompts investment and commitment prematurely."

Eryx shook his head. "A sad loss of life."

"Which we'll avoid with this project. The commission will test the lodestone before it's installed, of course. The date's set for an eight-day from now. But the small prototypes were proven safe, and the working stones are likely to be no different."

The two men plunged into a discussion of the esoteric details.

Liliyah noticed that her mama's attention wandered. Daymo Eryx had planted himself beside a charming mosaic mural, one of Mama's, in fact. It depicted a pebble strewn rivulet flanked by watercress and wild iris. Actual river stones combined with fragments of vivid glass and larger painted tiles.

Liliyah reached out her hand to touch the metallic sheen of a minnow. Its scales felt strangely warm. She sent a startled glance at her mother.

"I used chips of galena," Mama mused. "I wonder if I should try a creation entirely of metals; copper, tin, bronze, and lead. Could be an interesting composition . . ." Mama wasn't really paying her daughter any heed.

Liliyah closed her eyes and exhaled slowly, attempting to open her awareness to *energea*. Did a faint hum, that wasn't really a hum, but would be if *energea* were perceived through the ears instead of the mind, permeate the exhibition hall? She inhaled in preparation for another easy breath out. The aroma of sautéed fish croquettes threaded through the dominant florals of the perfumes and colognes worn by Navarys' wealthy and powerful, distracting Liliyah's focus. She was new to manipulating and perceiving *energea*. Like most children, her lessons in it had started soon after her celebration of her thirteenth natal day. Relax, she told herself. Yes, what was almost the lazy drone of a bumblebee lay on the air.

"Lili?" Papa's question interrupted her probing.

Liliyah's eyelids flew open.

"Let's go see the miniature." He touched her shoulder and gestured to an opening in the crowd.

She stepped forward.

The island of Navarys lay before her once again, this time at waist height on a tabletop stretching from the reflecting pool at one end of the hall to the sculpture of dolphins playing at the other. Comparing the diminutive landscape built by model enthusiasts to the real thing, she wondered if they too had experienced flight in one of the five Navarean airships. Navarys in miniature was so like Navarys from the air. Merely lacking the haziness provided by five hundred feet of air or the vivid brightness imparted by sunlight. She reached out to brush the spinning sails of a tiny windmill. *How –?* Oh! An *energea* stone – matte black and pebble-sized – capped its twirling roof, which propelled the drive shaft moving the sails.

"Ingenious, no?" came Papa's voice.

"But where is the fabrimancer operating the stone?" she wondered aloud.

"This is one of the new stones Daymo Mytris has been working on, the lodestones. They draw *energea* without the prompting of a human handler."

Liliyah felt her eyes widening. She turned away from the little miracle presented by the windmill to assess her father's feelings about it. His brows lifted slightly, and the corners of his mouth turned up. So this was for real. She thought immediately of her friend with the silk shop. Would the small crafters like Dama Omys have access to these lodestones? Imagine if a spinner could set one at the hub of her spinning wheel. Or a potter use one to move his potter's wheel. "Is it safe?" she blurted.

Papa's mouth straightened, not in tension, but in seriousness. "Yes. I tested it myself."

Liliyah's breath puffed out in a sigh of relief. Mago was wrong. His papa wasn't courting risky possibilities. She turned back to the miniature landscape. The gate to the model of the monarch's country palace had been mechanized with another of these lodestones, and its bronze filigree swung open and closed. Beyond the palace on another hillside, a tram drawing three carriages filled with nuggets of copper ratcheted along geared rails. This was the engine and the railway prompting this exhibition and reception. Going by the excitement of the public here tonight, the proposal would receive a quick approval.

Liliyah moved on around the table's edge, eager to see more of the intricate work of the modelers. Daymo Jeno was right. It *was* clever.

Closer to the city lay the aerodrome with the vaulted loggia where she'd disembarked just this afternoon and the four mooring towers, from one of which she'd crossed onto the *Subindo*. Instead of the spiral stair giving access to its top balcony and moveable gangway, a lift moved up and down the needle-nosed structure. Daymo Mytris would like that! She'd complained that climbing a hundred steps to get up to the airship was hard on her poor knees.

Sudden shadow fell across the aerodrome. *What?* Liliyah tilted her head toward the ceiling. Oh!

The model of an airship – not the *Subindo*, but the smaller *Ganador,* its silken covering vivid with magenta and royal blue stripes – drifted slowly down from overhead, controlled by yet another lodestone fastened to the bottom of its forward gondola. A thin, almost transparent guideline controlled the route the *Ganador* followed. Evidently its lodestone provided merely motive power to the propellers whirring on the side nacelles, not steering. Liliyah vented a quiet giggle. This was *energea*, after all, not fantasy!

Papa rested his hand on her shoulder, solid and comforting. "Pretty amazing, isn't it?"

Liliyah nodded. "And Daymo Mytris invented them? The lodestones?"

"He did, indeed. I'm proud to know him." Papa smiled at her quick glance. "And glad to live now. We're at a cusp of history, Lili. Our lives will change, probably unimaginably so. Can you guess what might be different?"

She couldn't, but found herself gazing across the miniature landscape to where Daymo Mytris stood receiving congratulations from a long line of guests eager to meet the great man. Dama Mytris posed at his side, gracious and welcoming, a nice counterpoint to her husband's slightly triumphant air. Where was Mago? Liliyah wondered uneasily. Surely his father would have liked him to participate in this celebration. *Papa can't be wrong.* But what if Mago was right? What if there were something to worry about?

She looked at Daymo Mytris again. Was his nose . . . different somehow? His color pale, compared to all the flushed and overheated people around him? She shook her head. *Papa's not wrong. He's never wrong.*

Next morning, Eirene woke her late.

"Wha' time izzit?" she murmured sleepily.

"Time for me to go to Dama Zario. She's joining a walking group today."

"Mmm?" Liliyah blinked and snuggled deeper into the silk of her quilts. The sun had warmed her bedchamber; she was seeking darkness, not escape from some long-gone dawn chill.

"Her physician told her the baby would be fine without her for an hour or two, but that she wouldn't be fine if she didn't get out of the house a little more and stretch her limbs." Liliyah could hear the smile in her old nurse's voice. "I must say I'm looking forward to having the little one to myself for a spell." Yes, Eirene did love babies.

Mago's words from yesterday came back to her. "You're only a baby anyway. With a nurse."

Liliyah sat up abruptly, snorting. She loved Eirene, but she didn't need her anymore. And even Mama couldn't bear to part with her. She'd become part of the family during all those years while Liliyah was little. And moped even amidst her pride when Liliyah outgrew the nursery and her nurse. Everyone was relieved when Dama Zario, a few doors down the hill, inquired whether Eirene could give her the mornings to help with the new baby. Win, win, win all round.

"I'm up," Liliyah announced, slithering out from under the net canopy that sheltered her bed.

The gauze of the window curtains tinted her room golden. It must be well past breakfast, if the sun had moved around the corner of the house that typically shaded her windows. She started scrambling out of her nightdress, rifling through the gowns on the wall pegs for something casual and comfortable.

"Now, sweetling, that's no way to go." Eirene's hand checked hers. "Your governess has indeed arrived in the schoolroom, but you've time to dress properly and eat." She gestured toward a tray resting on the low bench by the door. A bowl of berries, a pitcher of raisin kvass, and skewers of roast mutton sent tantalizing aromas into the air. Liliyah sniffed appreciatively – umm, she could almost taste the savory roasted meat – and slowed down enough to allow Eirene to tie her sash.

"Kiss the baby for me," she told her nurse as Eirene whisked herself away.

Lessons were ordinary, but interesting. The new math – algebra – was much more fun than mere calculation, and she'd always liked history, but studying *energea* – also new – was her current favorite. Her governess said that Liliyah was an aural practitioner, because she perceived the *energea* as sound. She couldn't imagine what it must be like for visual or kinesthetic fabrimancers. The musical tones resounding in her mind's ear felt so natural, so easy to compose the extensions that controlled their physical results. How would those who saw lattices of colored light or felt pressure on their limbs manipulate their *energea*? Her friend Cressy claimed to be a visual practitioner, but still. Liliyah tilted her head in puzzlement. People were so *different*! It was fascinating.

The afternoon found her in Cressy's shop. Liliyah had tried to persuade her mother to call on Dama

Mytris. She still wanted to question Mago in private. But Mama had her own plans.

"No, Lili. I'm walking with Hyacinthe, and looking forward to it, too. She's found a way to infuse essential lavender into clay tiles and promises to share the secret with me." Mama paused, scrutinizing Liliyah, then reaching out to tip her daughter's chin up. "You usually shirk formal visits, love. Why the sudden interest?" Her left eyebrow quirked up.

Liliyah felt her face heating and worked to meet her mother's curious gaze. "I wanted to ask Mago something."

Mama's eyes widened slightly. "Truly?" Her voice registered a teasing suggestiveness.

"He's an old friend, and yesterday reminded me that I missed him." Liliyah heard defensiveness in her own voice. But, really, how embarrassing that Mama thought she might like Mago *that* way. She didn't like anyone that way. Although Mago's newly broader shoulders had felt . . . nice against hers on the divan in the *Subindo*. She shivered, not in cold, but . . . unease.

"Well, Ione's busy entertaining the engineers from last night's gala in any case. We'll pay her a call in a few days." Mama's hand released Liliyah's chin to pat her cheek. "If you do indeed wish to see Mago."

Liliyah had acquiesced to the delay and headed out on her own more typical afternoon activity: visiting the shop owners on Neander Row. She'd started the habit young, asking questions of the clerks while in tow behind her nurse or her mother when they ran errands. The adults had laughed because her curiosity wasn't aimed at the sweet smells in the parfumiers, the music of the chimes in the garden shop, or the bright colors in the silk shop. She'd wanted to know how many units they kept in stock, what they paid to their suppliers compared to what they charged their customers, and all the other details of running a business. By the time she turned ten, Mama and Papa not only accepted her unusual interest, but encouraged it.

"She's got a gift for commerce," Papa declared. "Let her pursue it."

Now, at age thirteen, her afternoon interviews were commonplace.

The silk shop was one of her favorite stops. Its heavy, musky smell – exuded by the ornate brocades and the middle-weight velvets and the light gauzes alike – was associated with the ultimate pleasure in Liliyah's experience. Dama Omys had accepted Liliyah in some sort as a protégée and begun teaching her all the business savvy at her command. Liliyah got to inspect the financial records, the inventory lists, and the back storeroom. Plus Dama Omys had a young assistant who took to Liliyah the instant the girls were introduced. Cressy, three years older than Liliyah, possessed an equal fascination with commerce. She was intrigued by the possibilities of the new lodestones.

"Can you imagine putting one on the spooler that unwinds the filament from the silk cocoon? Instead of one fabrimancer per machine, you could have one per *six* machines! And he wouldn't have to use *energea* most of the time." Cressy bounced on her toes. "Every Navarean on the island will be rich!" she exclaimed.

"We're already rich," Liliyah insisted. "Compared to the mainlanders."

"Oh, mainlanders," scoffed Cressy. "Without *energea* . . ." her face sobered. "Dama Omys says their poor go hungry every winter. And it gets cold there!"

"I'm glad I was born here." Liliyah tried to imagine the chill of an ice-house continuing on for hours or days or months and failed. Visiting the underground space during a hot summer day felt good. It was less comfortable on that cool autumn morning last year, but she'd warmed up fast upon emerging with the ice chips she'd fetched to soothe her burnt tongue.

"I'd like to visit Imsterfeldt, though," mused Cressy. "Dama Omys says it has canals passing right through the city and town houses four and five stories tall!"

They'd moved on to talking about Liliyah's voyage on the *Subindo* and making plans to visit the dyer's manufactory next revel-day when shouting erupted in the allée outside, followed by running feet.

Liliyah broke off what she was saying to frown at Cressy, who frowned back. "What is it?" her friend worried.

Dama Omys was waiting on a customer purchasing vast amounts of heavy turquoise damask to curtain her drawing room windows. She looked up briefly to instruct the girls. "Go see what that's about, will you, please?"

Of the handful of passersby – early afternoon saw few shoppers – it was hard to get anyone to stop. One fat woman bustled up the stairs just above the shop's doorway, whimpering, "Oh, no! Oh, no!" under her breath, while three errand boys ran downhill, yelling, "Hurry! Hurry! Or you'll lose your place to the next fellow on the list!"

Liliyah turned to Cressy, eyes wide. "I don't know," Cressy answered her unspoken question. "It can't be good."

No, it felt bad. Which was scary and strange amidst the normal sensations of a spring day: sun warm on her cheek, cobblestones firm beneath her slippers, scent of almond flowers on the breeze. But something dreadful had happened, and something worse was coming.

His mother wasn't listening.

Mago gritted his teeth in frustration.

First Mater had explained that Pater was short on sleep. Next she'd insisted that he always sneezed in the spring, his lungs irritated by the pollens of orange blossom and almond. With all the seasonal chafing, of course his nose swelled.

"There's really no reason to worry, my dear," she repeated for the fourth time, and reached for the vial of nail enamel she'd set on the fountain coping beside her. Uncorking the diminutive vessel, she dipped a minute brush through the narrow neck, withdrew it carefully, and painted a broad stripe of emerald green on her thumbnail. She wrinkled her nose. The pine tar in its formula smelled unpleasantly.

Mago unclenched his jaw and looked away.

His father *had* been staying up late and rising early, frantically finishing last details on the massive loadstone that would power the engine transporting copper ore from the mines to the harbor. But Pater was experienced with deadlines. His temper had never grown quite so short-fused and volcanic for deadlines past. Why now? And his nose was more than swollen. It was changing shape. Something was wrong. Very wrong.

The breeze gusted strongly for an instant. Spray from the fountain misted his face, evaporating and cooling, then drying as the warmth of the sun prevailed. Mago stared at the horizon where sea met sky. Their house, just like its neighbors, fronted on a sloping allée punctuated by steps at the steepest stretches. But the walled courtyard behind the domicile occupied a slight bluff, giving him a more expansive view of the shore cliffs, rows of palms, and the tumble of mansions climbing this reach of Mount Sohlon. He sighed.

Was there any point in continuing this discussion? Mater would just defend Pater, no matter what he said, without answering his real question. He looked back to his mother, sitting on the wide curve of sandstone a little removed from him and concentrating on her grooming. Her hair gleamed blue black, and the skin of her throat emerged smooth from the upper drapery of her gown. She always seemed more poised than his friends' mothers. But right now the corners of her mouth crimped closed, and faint lines spread from the corners of her eyes. Two deeper lines marked the space between her brows.

She's worried, too, realized Mago. She's defending Pater from *her* accusations, not mine.

"Will he be normal again in the summer?" He hadn't meant to speak that fear aloud.

She set her nail brush back on its tray, re-corked the vial and clenched her fingers around it. "No. He won't."

Evaia below. Now he had her admission, he didn't want it. Wanted her false reassurance back. "What will we do?" he whispered.

Before she could answer, loud sobs broke from the open casements of the scullery. Shouts echoed in the allée. Their steward emerged from the house, his tread steady and majestic as always, despite the disturbance, as he crossed the sandstone flags of the courtyard. He stopped before Mago's mother. "Dama, there is news." His tone was even, his words unhurried. Why did Mago's stomach drop once more, falling again from the nadir produced by Mater's judgment of Pater?

"What is it?" Mater's tone was sharp.

"The sea bed shrugs its shoulders. Our monarch's own geomancer divines it."

Mater hunched as though punched in the gut. "Merciful deeps," she murmured. "It's the wave?"

"Yes, Dama."

"Mago! Come! We must get to the quay. Your father has sway with Daymo Zario. One of his galleys will carry us to safety." She started to her feet.

"There is time, Dama. And a governance."

"A governance? What governance? And how *much* time?"

"Eight turns of the glass. And a place by lot on a sea vessel or an airship."

"By lot?" Mater's nose pinched in, white, and her chin jerked up, outraged. "My husband is friend to the monarch and holds a seat in the first circle of merchants! How dare anyone deny his family by something so fickle as lot!"

Mago moved to grip his mother's forearm. She couldn't, she really mustn't, strike old Phyllos. He'd been with them from before Mago was born, and his dignity wouldn't stand the affront. Mater shook off her son's hand, recollecting herself.

"You have a place on Daymo Theniar's caravel, along with Daymo Mytris, Dama."

"And my son?" She looked haughty now, rather than alarmed.

"All children under fifteen years have a place, Dama." Did Phyllos' words possess a sardonic tinge?

Mater tossed her head. "Well, then, we must pack." Her brows knit. "Who has not a place?"

Phyllos bowed. "Our monarch has refused to depart until the last of his subjects is boarded. And . . . not all will board." The steward fell silent on the heels of this utterance, his demeanor stern.

No! Mater's mouth shaped the word. Mago felt his own do the same. But no sound issued forth.

Phyllos continued, "There are not places for all."

"No. There wouldn't be." Mater murmured, subdued. Then she rallied. "Mago, you will go to the quay now, while I direct the servants in their duties. Phyllos will accompany you." Her decision suffered a check. "Do *you* have a place, Phyllos?"

"Yes, Dama. I do, but –"

Mater looked shocked and relieved at once. "Good! Do you send a footman to Daymo Mytris and yourself take Mago to the caravel. Oh! And have another footman pull the travel trunks from storage. I'll start the maids to folding garments and swathing the heirloom china in padding –"

"Dama." Phyllo interrupted her. "The children are to be evacuated by airship, and Mago's place is on one of them. The *Subindo*."

Mago felt Mater's arm grope round his shoulders, trembling, while her lips shaped another silent no.

Why did his presence on the *Subindo* appall her? If the coming wave were so huge as to threaten all of Navarys, the seagoing vessels would also be threatened. The airships provided the safest berths. Thus their reservation for the island's children. Mago followed that logic perfectly. What was Mater thinking?

"I shan't part from my son!" she declared.

Phyllos' mouth quirked. "I fear you have little choice," he told her.

Liliyah paused in the atrium of her home.

Trunks, packing cases, and portmanteaus littered the marble floor. The servants' sandals slapped loudly as they hurried about their tasks. They barely noticed her, the daughter of the house, so focused were they on gathering valuables and stowing them. The head veil worn by one of the maids brushed Liliyah's cheek – an unwitting silken caress – as the young woman rushed by.

Mama appeared in the doorway to the front parlor. She stood straight, her eyes distant. Was she calculating what to leave and what to bring? Then she saw Liliyah. Her gaze warmed, and she surged forward to take Liliyah's hands. "You've heard? You know?"

Liliyah nodded, unspeaking. The messenger bearing the news had emerged from the shop next to Dama Omys' just as she and Cressy turned to go back inside.

"Mama . . . must we truly leave? Can a wave reach so high? All the way to the top of Mount Sohlon?"

Her mother's arm slipped over her shoulders, guiding her into the parlor, away from the bustle of the atrium. They sank onto the divan under the windows into the courtyard.

"We'll be safe, Liliyah. The ships will carry us away from danger. And we'll make new homes on the continent."

"Why can't we come back to Navarys? Back home. After the wave has passed?"

Mama sighed. "Our flocks and orchards will be swept away, love. How would we feed ourselves?"

Liliyah shrank into Mama's embrace. She'd been imagining massive ocean breakers overwhelming the quays, flooding the low-lying harbor streets. This new picture in her mind – trees uprooted and churned, goats and chickens submerged and drowned, a wave so immense as to be a mountain itself – presented disaster on another scale altogether.

"I'm scared," she whispered, then blushed. She should be strong, helping Mama choose and pack and get ready, not quivering like a baby and seeking comfort.

"It's a scary thing," agreed her mother. "Imagine if we had no geomancers." Liliyah shuddered. "But we do have them. And Navareans are wealthy. Even the poorest of us have resources enough to make a new start in Cambers or Solmondy. It will be an adventure!"

Liliyah felt her eyes widening. "Mama, you can't be looking forward to this!" Could she?

Mama managed a chuckle. "Well, no. But since we *must* do this, better to embrace it than resist it." She gave another squeeze to Liliyah's shoulders, then took her hands again. "Now. Can you choose your favorite trinkets and scrolls? I've packed my wardrobe, and I'd like to do my studio next. Do you need help?"

Liliyah bit her lip. Could she manage by herself? "No, I can do it," she decided. "I'll fold my gowns, too," she offered, "and wrap my sandals."

Mama patted her hand, hesitated, then forged ahead. "The weather's cooler on the continent. Pack all your warmer clothes, but only as many as will fit of your lightest gauzes and voiles. I've had two trunks placed in your chamber. One for clothing, one for toiletries and miscellany."

Liliyah clutched her mother's hand in sudden distress. "Dama Omys! Her silks! She can't possibly pack them all. Can I go help her? Will there be room on the ships for shop inventory?" The messenger had listed off baggage allowances and other practicalities, hadn't he? But she hadn't been listening, too confounded by his news, and Dama Omys had insisted she return home at once, before the messenger finished declaring all his tidings.

"The cargo holds are capacious enough," Mama answered. "It's time and –" Mama visibly swallowed . . . something "– it's time we lack."

"Please?"

Mama looked exasperated. "I'd rather you stay close." Her lips straightened. "Close to me."

"The Row's not far!"

"Lili." Mama's shoulders settled, and her voice chided.

Liliyah flushed.

Well, it wasn't far. Not really. Just three allées over and halfway down the hill. Of course it wasn't close either. But not clear across the city or down by the harbor.

"Liliyah." Mama sighed. "The city won't be . . . as safe as usual. When people are scared, they get angry. Sometimes violent. I want you close," she repeated.

Was that all? The tightness in Liliyah's chest eased. "One of the footmen could accompany me."

Mama tilted her head. Was she weakening?

"The hurly burly amongst the latecomers will be dangerous. The sooner we depart" – Mama's voice wobbled on that last word, then grew crisp – "the better."

"Will we go the instant your studio's packed?" Liliyah probed.

Mama's breath puffed out on a small laugh laugh. "I'm a fast packer. I'll be helping Hyacinthe as soon as I've finished here. Which . . . won't be long."

Ha! I've got her now. "If you're helping your friend, why can't I help mine?"

Mama's torso lost some of its rigidity. She reached out a hand and pinched Liliyah's chin. "Alright. Once you've packed your own things, you may help Dama Omys. But only two turns of the glass, mind." Her hand turned to cup Liliyah's cheek, cool and smooth and comforting. "And come straight home. Don't go to the aerodrome. Hear?"

What? Liliyah felt her forehead wrinkling. What did the aerodrome have to do with it?

"No, I won't. But . . . won't we go down to the harbor?"

"Oh!" Mama looked stricken. "Didn't the messenger say?"

Yet more anxiety fluttered Liliyah's stomach. Was there no end to the way dread piled atop dread piled atop dread?

"What is it?" Why had she asked? She didn't want to know.

"You're on the *Subindo*, love. All the children are. On the airships high above the wave and safe."

"Mama, no! I won't! I'll go with you and Papa. On the sea. Please!"

Mama bent and kissed her brow. "Go pack!"

Mago stood uneasily before the lodestone.

It was matte black, a flattened oval nearly the size of his own head, and resting on a limestone pedestal. Did an air current flow off it? No, but there was something. Mago closed his eyes.

The fluting of a single bird floated through the open windows of the workshop, accompanied by the wafting perfume of the clematis vine. Mago extended his arms along with his sense of *energea*. He was a kinesthetic practitioner – a beginning one – and felt this invisible power through touch and pressure. Was the tide off the lodestone *energea*? It surely wasn't air.

Ah! Energea, indeed!

The hairs on his forearms rose. A heaviness pressed against the whole front of his body, even while an ache awakened in his bones and surged up through his skin, a stinging prickle, passing outward to the lodestone. Mago gasped.

"Get away from there!" Swift, hard footsteps followed the shout, and then his father's angry grip jerked Mago backward. He stumbled, working to get his feet under him, and overbalanced into Pater's chest. Together they slammed into something, and Mago's eyes flew open. He grabbed for the work table's edge, missed, and plummeted. The grasp on his shoulder brought him to an abrupt halt just above the floor, nose to brick. Apparently Pater had kept his feet.

Next instant, Mago had his feet, too, hauled upright by Daymo Mytris.

"How dare you jeopardize my genius? My workshop is not your play patch! What are you doing here?" Pater's face darkened with rage.

Mago opened his mouth to reply. Closed it again. This made no sense. He'd often watched his father work before. Always been welcome in his workshop. His mind flashed to his question – asked just one turn of the glass ago – and to Mater's answer. *Will he be normal again? No.* This was not normal.

"I could help you pack up your tools," Mago suggested.

Pater's brows drew down farther. "Unnecessary." Which was true. One need merely lock the latches to the chests, and footmen could carry them to the caravel's cargo hold. "You'll go to your mother and do as she tells you. Now."

But Mater wouldn't be at home. She'd departed for the palace, determined to pester the monarch for a place for her son by her side on the sea-going caravel. She'd sent him to help his father. Who was sending him back. But now was no time to argue. Mago saw that clearly enough.

"What do you wait for?" demanded Pater. "Get out!"

Mago got.

The allée outside the workshop traversed a particularly steep slope of the mountain. It was all steps and landings, too precipitate for a ramped roadway. Pair after pair of liveried footmen tramped down the stairs with heavy trunks. Pater was not the only tenant moving the contents of his workshop to the harbor. Mago descended a dozen steps, then dodged aside to allow a bulky packing crate manhandled by six porters to pass before him. He glanced back at the workshop door to see Palujon Clisto knocking on its panels. What?

The door opened swiftly, Daymo Clisto stepped inside, and the door closed behind him.

Huh! Mago started to follow in the wake of the massive packing crate, then stepped back into the nook where he'd squeezed himself out of the way.

Why was Palujon Clisto seeking out Mago's father, someone he deliberately avoided? And why had Pater admitted him inside the workshop?

Mago paused a moment longer, then turned uphill rather than down.

I'm going to find out.

He climbed beyond the workshop door, then turned into a narrow passage between buildings, worming around a forgotten trash bin and then under a low drainpipe. Through an ell bend, down one step, jump over a cellar opening, and then up three steps. Around the next corner lay the courtyard adjacent to Pater's workshop. Mago slowed and edged along the wall toward the nearest open window. He stopped beside the lattice supporting the clematis. No need to get closer. Neither Pater nor Clisto was keeping his voice low.

"You spurn me when my research suffers few results and now court me when it prospers. Why would you expect my welcome under such circumstances?" Pater sounded scornful.

Clisto's reply remained moderate. "This is not about me. Or about you. I speak on behalf of our children. Your son and his friends. My nieces and nephews. All the young ones of Navarys."

"Mere diversion," scoffed Pater. "You seek to steal my work, my ideas! I know your sort: unable to devise your own creations, parasitic on those of others. Surely your cunning suggested better avenues than approaching me directly!"

Did Palujon sigh? If so, the puff of breath huffed too softly for Mago to hear it. "I intend no deception, Daymo Mytris. My motive and its reason are exactly as I've stated them. I beg you reconsider."

"My victory, my triumph, my hard-won success. You expect me to simply give it to you for the asking? You must be mad!"

"Not to me," urged Palujon. "To posterity and its vulnerable couriers. Our children, Daymo!"

"You have none!"

Was that pause another sigh? Mago crept closer to the window, scrunching his neck forward to avoid the tickling leaves of the clematis vine. He crouched and edged an eye above the low sill. Both men stood tensely, confronting one another over the pedestal where lay the large lodestone. Palujon Clisto held his chin very level and his shoulders straight, as though physical restraint might support verbal moderation. Pater crouched slightly, almost ready for attack? Or . . . as though ill?

Was Pater ill?

Mago scrutinized him: flushed but with a sallow undertone, faint redness to the eyes, a trifling distortion to his features. These were no symptoms Mago had ever heard of. But – *he's sick. I just know he is.* And now he sounded like Liliyah yesterday, just knowing things because. *I'll have to tell her she was right.* Sometimes a person *did* just know. But what could he do for Pater? How could he help him? What was wrong with him?

Palujon reached out his hand, palm up. "Daymo Mytris, for pity's sake." His voice pleaded, rather than commanded.

Pater took the gesture utterly wrong and hit out, knocking Clisto's arm aside, then stepping around the lodestone pedestal to push his visitor roughly toward the exit. "You trespass on my property and good nature alike. Be gone from here!"

Palujon wasn't ready to give up. He stepped away from his attacker, sufficiently nimble to avoid Pater's follow-up swing, but stopped before the door onto the allée. "Daymo, I ask only your small prototypes! And only as a loan! You may keep your . . . your . . . masterpiece" – why did Clisto hesitate over that word? – "entirely within your own purview. Although 'twere better in the deepest depth of the ocean."

Those last words, muttered low, were a mistake. Pater had regained self-control, but he opened the workshop door and coldly bowed Daymo Clisto out. If borrowing the exhibition lodestones were as important as Palujon pretended, he'd failed.

Mago, still crouching, turned, resting his back against the rough stucco of the wall, and slid down to sit on the courtyard flags. Palujon seemed a reasonable man. That was why Mago had sought his opinion yesterday on the *Subindo*. Pater was the unreasonable one. But why *did* Palujon want Pater's lodestones? Especially now, amidst the evacuation of all Navarys? Surely whatever it was could wait. Perhaps Pater was right in assigning nefarious motives to the aeromancer. Perhaps Pater wasn't unreasonable; just irritable because he was ill.

A strong thumb and forefinger pinched Mago's ear, drawing him painfully to his feet. "Go. Home." Pater's anger, chilled under its suppression prior to Clisto's departure, grew icy. "Now."

But Mago possessed no history of fearing his father, and he refused to begin one now. "Pater, why does Daymo Clisto want your lodestones? His concern seemed genuine!"

Pater's rigid jaw relaxed, and he released Mago's ear. "You heard it all?"

"No. Just the last bit. About the evacuating children being in danger."

"They'll be safe enough once they're on the airships. Clisto's seizing this misfortune to test some ideas he's developing for combining aeromancy with my invention. Cold-blooded opportunist!" Pater shook his head. "I can see it now: The *Subindo* and the *Ganador* arrive at Imsterfeldt as planned, while the *Belezea* and the *Magnifikat* go astray somewhere to the south, Istria maybe. And Daymo Clisto is the richer by two lodestones." Pater snorted. "A loan! I think not!"

"He intended to attach the lodestones to the airship engines? In place of the *energea* stones?" probed Mago.

"The engines?" Pater sounded surprised. He paused, then opened the paned door next to the window, and ushered Mago inside. "No, the fins and elevator control surfaces. To increase the stability of the ship before the wind."

Mago felt his eyebrows crinkling.

Pater locked the courtyard door and placed its key on the nearby hook. "Didn't you realize the airships are extremely vulnerable to gusts? They present an enormous area to air movement, like a great sail.

They're far more susceptible to weather than sea vessels, you know."

No, Mago hadn't known. But, if that were true, could Palujon's worry be real? "Then shouldn't the children go in the caravels, the adults take the airships?"

"Were we facing a hurricane, indeed yes, but we face a wave, son." Pater's voice gentled, losing all remnants of his chilly anger. "Speaking of which –" he placed a hand on Mago's shoulder and gave it an affectionate jostle "– are you ready to board?"

"Mater sent the footmen with the household crates down to the quay half a glass ago. They'll be here for your tool chests soon, I expect."

"Good. Very good." Pater pulled a small crate next to the pedestal with the lodestone and pried its lid upward. Mago stepped forward to help shift the stone itself, but Pater checked him. "I need no help here. Do you have a satchel packed for the airship? I know the allowance is scant, but you'll need a few items."

Mago nodded.

Pater gripped his forearm. "Then help me thusly: detach the prototype lodestones from their engines in the exhibition hall and pack them in this." He lifted a small wallet with five pockets and a buckled strap securing it closed. "Let your mater place it in her reticule. Can you do that?"

Mago nodded again. He'd done quite a bit of manipulating the small lodestones with Pater before things had gotten so strained between them. *He does trust me. I wonder why . . .* Had it been fear, not anger, that so provoked his father earlier? Mago tucked the wallet into the pocket beneath his belt and moved toward the allée door.

"Mago?"

He paused. Pater's arm wrapped round his shoulders and snugged him in close. Mago glanced up in surprise. Were Pater's eyes the tiniest bit shiny? "The caravels will be some weeks slower than the airships. This is goodbye, for a time."

Mago felt his throat tighten. He turned into his father's embrace and hugged him hard. "I love you, Pater."

Pater's hold strengthened, then let him go. "Tell your mater I'll be along shortly to accompany her to the quay. But don't you wait for me. As soon as you've given her the prototypes, have Phyllos escort you to the aerodrome. No sense in risking the mobs likely to gather later in the day."

The exhibition hall lay on the far side of the city from Pater's workshop, but at nearly the same elevation. Mago climbed two flights of stairs, feeling the pull in his thighs from their tall risers, to a little-travelled lane cutting across the slope of the mountain. Ranks of flowering almond trees generated a speckled shade, pleasantly aromatic, but the usual quietude was missing. Pageboys carrying messages, porters transporting luggage, families locking their front gates and departing, a bachelor delaying to help an elderly relative make sure the curling tongs really were packed at the bottom of a valise: the scene was busy. Although not panicked, or even hectic, Mago noted. The citizenry moved with dispatch, but calm purpose prevailed thus far.

"Mama! Jaffy go boat!" piped a toddler's voice. His wool-stuffed toy giraffe made ocean wave swoops in his hands.

"No, no," corrected his mother. "Jaffy go flying!"

"Ooooh!" squealed her son.

Mago smothered a grin. Pray Evaia the kid was on the *Ganador* or the *Belezea*, not the *Subindo*. Mago didn't want to be present when he discovered neither his mama nor his nurse would be accompanying him into the air. Of course, the *Subindo* would likely have its own complement of crying infants. Phyllos had claimed that each grown woman aboard the airship would have ten or even fifteen young ones under her protection. Most of the kids would be missing their usual caretakers. Mago grimaced. Maybe Mater would succeed in getting him a berth on a sea-going vessel.

Every single one of the many doors into the exhibition hall were locked. *Huh.* What to do next? Return to Pater for a key? Did Pater *have* a key?

Mago checked the attached box office where tickets were sold when an exhibition wasn't free or invitation-only. Not surprisingly, it was empty of the clerk. But the lower sash of the sales window hung open by a hair's width. Mago tested the bronze frame. Loose! He pushed, and the sash slid upward. Ah, ha! Nipping in through the opening, nabbing a key from the several hanging on a rank of hooks, and scrambling back out again took less than two grains falling in the glass. Mago pushed the sash all the way down after his exit, but the catch – inside the glass – perforce stayed unfastened.

He hurried under the hall's portico.

"Mago!" someone called from the allée. Who? He whipped his head around to see.

Liliyah scurried up the portico steps to him, slightly breathless, an even more breathless (and burdened) footman behind her.

"Are you assigned to the *Subindo*? Your house steward said so. I thought we could walk to the aerodrome together." She smiled hopefully.

"Yes, but –" Mago cut himself off. He didn't know that Mater would succeed on her errand to the monarch. "Yes."

"I'm not quite ready. That is, *I'm* ready, but I'm still helping Dama Omys pack up her shop."

Mago frowned. Dama Omys? He dredged his memory. Oh, yes. The proprietor of the silk shop where Liliyah pursued an informal apprenticeship in business practices.

"I'm helping my pater pack up his inventions," he offered in return. Then fitted the key into its lock, turned it, and swung the door open. Liliyah came with him, but her footman, carrying too many parcels, sank onto a bench outside.

It was immediately obvious that something was wrong. No crowds hid the vast table supporting the miniature landscape, where an unnatural absence gaped. The pressure generated by the five lodestones – pressure which Mago, as a kinesthetic fabrimancer, should feel right now – was gone.

"Oh!" exclaimed Liliyah. "The humming! Where is it? It's too quiet!"

Mago looked at her, puzzled.

"I'm an aural practitioner," she explained.

Of course. Just as he should feel the lodestones, she should hear them.

Mago walked forward to examine the denuded landscape, Liliyah in his wake.

He'd expected the gears to the driveshafts to be disengaged. It wouldn't make sense to leave the tram scooting up and down the mountain or the windmill spinning unwatched. Mechanical devices required supervision, even small non-serious ones. But not only were the gears disengaged, the lodestones powering them had been removed, and the model airship, deflated of the gas that kept it aloft, draped its bright silk over one of the mooring masts.

Mago checked the aerodrome lift and the palace gate, and then the shelves in the storage room, but not one lodestone remained on the premises. He turned to Liliyah, still dogging his footsteps and looking as deflated as the airship, as deflated as he felt.

"Someone's stolen them!" It seemed incredible. Who would do such a thing? And why? Surely they had more important things to do now, on the cusp of disaster. His pater's words came back to him. *The* Belezea *and the* Magnifikat *go astray somewhere to the south. And Daymo Clisto is the richer by two lodestones.*

Mago reached to grip Liliyah's shoulders. "Daymo Clisto! Pater was right!"

Liliyah drew back, eluding Mago's touch. Her chin jutted. "I liked Palujon," she insisted.

"But he asked Pater for these lodestones. Just now he asked him. Liliyah, he must have taken them. He *begged* Pater to lend them. And Pater said no."

"Why did he want them?"

Mago shook his head. "I have to get them back. They're Pater's life work. And it's not right! Not right that Daymo Clisto uses the disorganization of the evacuation to steal from him." Mago felt his teeth gritting together. "Help me, Lili! Where would I find Clisto?"

Liliyah bit her lip. "Mago . . . I don't know. I'm not sure you're right. Maybe we should be helping Palujon. I still trust him. And I don't –" she stopped. Looked down. Looked back up. "Mago, even you were worried that your pater was making a bad mistake."

He had been. Somehow he wasn't anymore. Pater's irrational anger, familiar across the last year, but previously foreign, should increase his worry. But it hadn't. "My pater is sick," he announced. "Not crazy. And I trust *him*." Would Liliyah understand? Would she agree? Her lips straightened.

"I saw him," she confessed.

Mago leaped on her words. "Clisto? When? Where? Oh, tell me!"

"The tinkers' bazaar. Persuading the vendor of essential oils to unpack one of his crates in order to sell a vial of perfume or something to him. But, Mago, I can't go with you! I have to finish helping Dama Omys." She hesitated, then burst out: "And I'm still not sure you're right!"

They parted then. She to return to Neander Row, while her footman made a trip to the quays. Mago to seek Daymo Clisto in the bazaar, firmly quashing the sense of misgiving that lurked under his certainty.

Bidding Mama farewell was hard. *Not* bidding Papa goodbye was harder.

The mood of the streets had changed, from urgent orderly bustle to more turbulent activity tinged with edgy anger. Hurrying pageboys no longer apologized when they jostled elderly matrons. Fathers shepherding families bore frowning faces and a willingness to shove through the crowd. Lengthening afternoon shadows sheltered lurkers with hard, avaricious eyes. Perhaps one of them had stolen Daymo Mytris' lodestones. Liliyah moved closer to her mother, clutching her arm and inhaling comfort from the faint sweetness that clung to Mama's skin, even on the heels of sweaty packing and too many trips up the ladder to their neighbor's attics.

Mama patted Liliyah's hand, but kept her eyes on their surroundings. "Almost there, love."

Reaching the refuge of the air terminal brought relief from the sense of risk, but ushered in a different distress. Infants wailed or sobbed. School-age kids played pranks and started impromptu games of tag. Nursemaids scolded. Worried parents issued last moment instructions or folded their offspring close in anguished embrace. All Navarys parted from their loved ones.

Liliyah stopped dead just inside the great front portal, and the merchant behind her, towing twins, vented a curse, "Evaia below!" before dodging around to one side.

Mama stepped behind a column out of the flow of arriving evacuees. Liliyah reached for her mother's cheek, sculpted and silken under her palm. "Mama, please come with me. Or let me come with you."

Mama drew her in close, bent to touch her forehead to Liliyah's, and smoothed Liliyah's hair. "It's alright. I promise."

"Mama, how can it be alright? Dama Omys says the wave is so huge it will drown Mount Sohlon. Your ship will be crushed!"

Mama's laugh sounded low and encouraging. "The wave grows as the ocean bottom rises to the shallows. Far out to sea, it's very, very broad – many leagues – but so low none of us on shipboard will even notice it."

"Truly?"

"Truly. 'Tis the ships still in harbor that will be lost, and the ones near shore, threatened." Mama squeezed Liliyah's hands. "So. The sooner we get you in the air and me on the water, the better."

The terminal clerks had lists and procedures. The *Belezea*, the *Ganador*, the *Magnifika*, and the *Azulinike* were tethered from the mooring towers, but Liliyah's berth was on the *Subindo*. That largest airship was tied down beside the upper loggia. Had it been it only yesterday she'd disembarked there?

Registered with the clerk tallying evacuees and the one tallying airship assignments, permissions granted by Mama, and her satchel weighed and approved, Liliyah followed the temporary rope handrail to the grand staircase connecting the concourse to the mezzanine, then stopped again. She turned and threw her arms around her mother, felt Mama's arms encircling her. There were no words. Mama's cheek pressed the top of Liliyah's head.

"I love you," Mama murmured.

Liliyah clung tighter.

Mama chuckled. "It's now, sweet."

Liliyah gulped, nodded, and backed up to the first step. "You tell that shipmaster he better do a good job." She thrust her chin forward. "For me!"

Mama laughed – with, not at her. "I've already reminded *Subindo's* captain that his cargo surpasses the worth of the monarch's treasury a thousand fold." Her face sobered. Her forefinger traced Liliyah's jaw. "Go!"

Liliyah went.

Mago rebounded off the broad back of a shopkeeper, teetered at the top of half a dozen steps, clutched for the railing that wasn't there, felt wisteria leaves brushing the nape of his neck as he started to fall, and grabbed the twisting bark of its trunk just in time.

"Watch it, you!" he yelled, adding his voice to the shouts of other jostled pedestrians.

The shopkeeper grunted, pulled his hand cart from the narrow side passage, reversed his direction, and trundled over to a ramp adjacent to the the stairs. "Watch your own self," he tossed over his shoulder and turned the corner.

Mago shook his fist, then his head. No point in recriminations. The man was gone, and he wasn't the only one paying less heed to courtesy or care. Any folk who didn't make it to the quays within the next glass or two would find the ships had sailed without them.

"You okay, young 'un?"

Mago let go of the wisteria and swiveled to see a man with a blanket-bundled child cradled against his shoulder with one arm, the other arm reaching to steady Mago. The man's wife, behind and below him on the steps, had a pinched, anxious face and two more children in tow.

"I'm okay," Mago reassured him. He looked up and down the allée. No other family groups in sight. Most mothers and fathers had long since gotten their offspring to the airships and themselves to the caravels. "Are *you* okay?" Maybe *they* needed help. The little boy huddled in the blanket looked sick.

The man jerked his head no. "Calpurnia has a place on the *Subindo* with our son. We'll be alright." His eyes grew stern. "But you're headed the wrong way to the aerodrome, lad. Are you here with leave from your parents?"

Uh, oh. Mago was going to find himself ushered willy nilly home or aboard the *Subindo*, if he couldn't come up with a convincing explanation. This father was clearly the ultra responsible type, ready to see a stranger to safety even amidst his own difficulties.

"I'm fetching my pater's *energea* stones. My pater's Daymo Mytris," he informed the man. Would that work? Most Navareans knew of Mago's father. "One of the engineers took them home from the exhibition hall, and Pater wants to pack them now." There. Almost the truth.

The man's expression lightened. "Don't be too long about it, young 'un. Which ship are you on?"

Mago suppressed a sigh. "The *Subindo*."

"I'll tell 'em you're on your way." He patted Mago's back. "Hurry!"

Mago nodded – "I will" – and strode briskly uphill. The tinker's bazaar lay near the harbor, but he didn't want to follow this family downhill. Daymo "Responsible" might easily change his mind about letting Mago alone. *I'll just cut over to the Athanacles Terrace and walk down that way.*

The bazaar was largely empty, a littered expanse of stone flagging under dim canvas, with one last vendor packing up and another handing four portmanteaus to a footman. The scent of grilled meats lingered, reminding Mago that it was tea time. On any other day, he'd be at home, sipping chilled peach nectar and nibbling cucumber sandwiches. He could almost taste the peaches, feel the crunch of the cucumber under his bite. His stomach stirred. The midday nuncheon was long past.

The footman loaded two of the bags on his shoulders, the straps crisscrossing his torso. He bent to grab the other two with his hands and staggered toward the entrance, the vendor in his wake. Wait! That was the perfume vendor. No wonder the footman lurched as he walked. Four cases full of glass vials must be beyond heavy.

Mago moved to block the bazaar's entrance. "Sir, a moment of your time. Please!"

The vendor frowned. "I don't have a moment, and neither do you," he said.

"I'm trying to find Daymo Clisto. I heard he had purchased a vial of scent from you. Just a glass past."

The vendor snorted. "Glue, not perfume. And I don't know where he went after. Now, scat!"

Mago found himself moving aside since the pair didn't stop. "Please!"

"Try Daymo Ramias, if you must." The vendor frowned harder. "But you'd best wait till you arrive in Imsterfeldt, lad. It's late for doing ought but boarding your airship." And he strode outside, shaking his head.

Daymo Ramias, Daymo Ramias, who? *Oh, I know. He's another aeromancer.* But where . . . ? Basilia Row? Yes. Basilia Row.

Mago sprinted.

The last pull to Daymo Ramias' home was extra steep. Thighs burning, he dropped onto a bench under a flowering almond. The breeze had died, and the tree's aroma hung as a palpable presence on the still air. Mago peered farther up the slope. Which house was it? The one with the lemon stucco? Or the mint stucco? Or – ?

The door to the domicile between the two, more modest in size, but opulent with a limestone facade, opened. And Palujon Clisto stepped out.

Burning muscles not withstanding, Mago leapt from his bench. Up, up, up! Would he catch him? Faster!

But the two men were shaking hands. Clisto passed something very small to his colleague. A lodestone! Then Daymo Ramias went back inside and shut the door. Daymo Clisto departed the front stoop, striding briskly, then breaking into a run. Did he suspect he was followed? Mago attempted more speed, reaching the top of the steep stretch with wobbly legs just as his quarry nipped around a corner. Gah! His command to his own limbs for another sprint produced three faltering steps. Mago subsided to a walk, but kept going. *If I can just keep him in sight.*

The gentle slope up to the intersection felt harder even than the steeper hill prior to it. Mago paused, panting and puffing, feeling droplets of sweat trickling along his temples. He leaned against the stucco of the lemon house. *Must. Keep. On.* No one paid him any heed. Three couriers dashed by him, undeterred by the hill, headed for the palace. They met and sidestepped a gang of wild-looking young men tramping down. One thrust out a foot to trip the rearmost courier, who simply bounded over it.

"What a wuss!" jibed the youth's companion, a puffy-eyed fellow with a nasty leer. "You missed!"

"I'll get the next idiot going up instead of down," replied his friend.

"No you won't."

"Will."

"Na, uh. I will!" sneered the puffy-eyed one.

"Wager you?"

"Done!"

Evaia below. I'm the next idiot going up. Mago staggered away from the lemon stucco propping him, slipped behind the water trough at the corner, and hustled along the level cross way. A couple supervising three porters hurried by, shielding him from the intersection behind. He glanced back. The bullies had passed. But where was Clisto? Mago searched the alleé ahead. A large elderly matron harangued her diminutive husband over a pile of valises and three trunks, while a crone screeched at them to clear the blocked way. Two porters shoved the luggage roughly aside, ignoring the husband's pleas that they add his baggage to their load.

Mago attempted a jog. Yes! His legs could manage that much, at least. He passed the stranded trio, following the curve of the alleé. The street was emptying rapidly, the last laggards heading down toward the harbor and their transport away from Navarys. A smooth head bobbed above the crush at the next intersection. Clisto! Mago sped his heavy feet, then slowed to thread through the clot of people, bags, and a broken crate with spilled household goods surrounding it.

He slowed further in the next deserted stretch of the alleé. A bunch of ruffianly types clustered beside a front stoop. What? Oh! They were wrenching open the bars of a cellar window. Thieves!

Mago stopped altogether. Should he rush forward and yell? Or turn right around and rush away? Did it really matter, given that the absent householder had chosen to abandon whatever was left in the dwelling?

The question became moot when three burly marshals emerged from an adjacent side channel and collared the burglars. Literally. Each law enforcer grabbed two thieves by the hair, banged their heads together, and tossed the culprits toward the next corner with an alleé aimed downhill.

Clisto darted out from a farther side channel, following in the wake of the thwarted housebreakers. Did he have business with them? Mago started forward.

"Hold up, lad." One of the marshals stepped in front of him. "You shouldn't be here."

Mago trotted out his earlier excuse. "I'm on an errand for my pater, Daymo Mytris."

"Then you shouldn't be." The marshal's eyes narrowed. "Nikos, peel off and escort this lad to the aerodrome. The ships will lift soon, but you should just make it in time to get him aboard." His meaty hand felt heavy on Mago's shoulder. "Which airship were you assigned to?"

Mago drew back, but the marshal's grip was firm. "The *Subindo*. But –"

"Nay, lad. I don't want your story."

"But –"

"We've heard them all. Nikos?" And the marshal manhandled him into the grip of his colleague, the said Nikos, returning from the crossway down which they'd dispatched the thieves.

"But a thief stole my pater's *energea* stones. I have to get them back!"

"No time for that, son. Your father'll have to chose between you and his stones. I'm thinking he'd chose you. And if he wouldn't, well, we're here, and he isn't." Nikos tilted his chin up. "Who did you say your father was, son?"

"Daymo Mytris. The famous inventor." Could he persuade these men to help him catch Clisto? "Please! Palujon Clisto covets my father's renown, and it's not fair! These are the *new* stones, the lodestones, and they belong to my father."

"I'd heard . . . something." Nikos grimaced. "Wait a moment . . . He's that aeromancer. The one who advises the monarch." Nikos' grip on Mago's shoulder tightened. "That's quite an accusation, son."

Nikos' supervisor intervened. "Never mind. I'll pass an all-points directive to question Daymo Clisto – *politely* – should he sighted." The man's gaze sharpened. "Which I doubt! Only malefactors left now. Reasonable folk are long gone. Except this boy here who *should* be gone."

Mago squirmed.

"Nikos! Move him along."

And Nikos did.

Liliyah's legs felt heavy as she climbed the stairs from the concourse to the mezzanine. Head down, she watched the marble treads pass under her reluctant footsteps and wished, *wished*, she could have seen Papa. He'll be safe, she told herself. *Mama said.* He's on the caravel now. *I'll see him in a fortnight.* But she wasn't sure she believed it.

Murmured goodbyes and muffled sobs floated up from the children and parents bidding one another farewell. Shouts from the ground crew outside intruded from the open loggia above. Liliyah could smell the blau gas used to power the auxiliary engines of the airship, volatile and acrid in her nose. Her right foot slapped the top tread of the stairs, her left, the marble floor of the loggia's gallery. She looked up.

Yesterday, the *Subindo* had sailed from a mooring tower, with room for only one gangway connecting the tower's balcony to the airship's gondola. And Liliyah hadn't looked back when she disembarked here at the air terminal. The airship filled the view through the loggia's archways completely. Each arch displayed the polished wood of *Subindo's* gondola and, above that, its varnished canvas of royal blue silk adorned by the monarch's golden heraldry: two unicorns rampant balancing a shooting star on their horns. Three gangways touched the gondola midships, and a short line of children waited at each one. Was that Cressy? Liliyah hurried to the forward gangway.

"Cressy!"

The girl looked toward Liliyah, then looked away again. Not Cressy. Liliyah felt her cheeks heat. Of course. Cressy was just a year too old to ride an airship. She'd be on one of the caravels, sailing west asea. Although the stranger's shiny brown curls were gathered in the exact same topknot as Cressy's, with the exact same twist of green ribbon. There was some excuse for Liliyah's mistake.

A flight attendant stood just inside the gondola doorway with yet another list. She located Liliyah's name on the second page, checked it off, and directed Liliyah to the spiral stair nearer the bow of the gondola. The sitting area – was it really just yesterday she'd perched on that divan? – remained empty of passengers. Likely it would fill later.

The second floor of the gondola featured four gracious dining chambers and a dumbwaiter connecting them to the kitchens located within the skin of the framework holding the airship's gas bags. Harried serving staff ferried platters to noisy eight- and nine-year-olds arguing about whether they liked the food or not. The scent of pea soup made Liliyah swallow. She could see the thick cream swirled over the savory, green liquid. Yum. But a flight attendant motioned her toward another spiral stair. Even with all the extra chairs crowded around the tables, the evacuees would have to eat in shifts.

The third floor of the passenger quarters, with the kitchens aft and the staterooms fore, proved to be Liliyah's destination. She checked the number over the door of the nearest stateroom, thirty-four, and started down that corridor. Thirty-five, thirty-six, thirty-seven – oh! A plump woman backed out of thirty-eight, bounced against Liliyah, and turned abruptly to embrace her.

"Eirene!" It was amazing how good it felt to see a familiar face.

"Sweetling! Oh!" Eirene's arms tightened, then released her. She studied Liliyah's face a moment, then smiled and drew forward a little tot of about three years of age. "Neoma needs to tinkle. Could you take her to the ship's head at the end of the hall?"

Before Liliyah could answer, a cry sounded from within the stateroom. "No! No! No! Mama said it's *mine*. She *gave* it to me! Ow!" Eirene dove back through the door, leaving Neoma staring dubiously at Liliyah.

"I'm Lili," Liliyah introduced herself. Noting Neoma's crossed and twisting legs, she held out her hand and suggested, "Let's go see what *Subindo* has in the way of chamberpots, shall we?"

Neoma stared a moment longer, then grabbed Liliyah's hand, and tugged her forward.

Airship chamberpots turned out to be very sophisticated. A tank above the pot released water through a pipe that cleared the pot after use via a central outlet, the waste disappearing, perhaps to a holding tank. Interesting, and more comfortable than she'd expected. Most of Navarys used sun composting, which wouldn't be practical in the air.

Returning Neoma to stateroom thirty-eight, Liliyah discovered Eirene involved in shepherding three more toddlers waking from their naps. There were only two bunks – tight quarters – but the little ones were small enough to fit with their heads on a pillow at each end. Eirene produced Pago and Juliya puppets on sticks from beneath the lowest bunk, handed them to Liliyah, and left her to it. Three other staterooms full of children, two of whom were infants, lay under Eirene's care. Liliyah, poised for protest, accepted the puppets and nodded. Right. Despite her calm and purposeful demeanor, Liliyah's nurse was flustered. And no wonder! Eirene loved children, but sixteen were too many for anyone, even an expert!

Liliyah raised the Juliya puppet upright and pulled the line that flapped its mouth. She made her voice shrill. "You're a bad boy! Bad! I won't let you hit me!" And she flailed the puppet's arms, lifting the Pago puppet to receive his sister's blows.

Mago glanced aside to a narrow passage blocked by listing rubbish bins. A noisome rankness hung over the cranny, but if he darted in there, he'd just fit between the near bin and the wall, and the marshal – wouldn't.

Nikos' meaty hand, absent for the last hundred paces, descended on Mago's shoulder and gripped. Had he been so obvious?

"No you don't, son. Not worth it. Why are you so set on missing *Subindo's* departure?"

Mago searched the allée ahead. The steep slant of its cobbles punctuated by irregular stairs remained utterly vacant of distractions he could use to escape his escort. Was the entire city empty? That was the idea, he supposed. Withdraw every last Navarean from the island to a caravel or an airship. But hadn't Mater said not all would board? No, that was Phyllos. Was he right? Weren't the other two marshals completing a final pass through the upper alleés, rounding up stragglers, before they sought their own berths at sea? Who could elude them? *I didn't.*

"Mago!"

Mater's voice pealed from the hill behind him. "Marshal Nikos, wait!"

Her tone commanded.

Nikos halted and swung around, his fingers still clamped on Mago's person. "Yes, dama?"

Mago burst into speech. "Mater, he won't let me go! And I've got to go. Pater sent me after the lodestones in the exhibition hall, but Palujon Clisto's stolen them!"

Mater's gaze grew stern. "You know this?"

"I saw him give one to Daymo Ramias."

"Ah!" She shifted her focus to the marshal. "Mago is accurate, daymo. These lodestones belong to my husband. They are valuable, representing many years of research and labor. It is your duty to prevent their theft and restore them to their rightful owner."

Nikos cleared his throat. "Begging your pardon, dama, but my duty belongs to the monarch, and he commands that I push every Navarean I can find onto a boat or an airship as fast as I can manage. No exceptions. They've even dredged up a forgotten derelict to make places for the folk who lost the lottery."

Mater's nose tipped back, and she stared down it. "You tell me, you, a guardian of the law, that you condone thievery and assault? I can't believe my ears!" How did she achieve that regal inflection?

Nikos shuffled his feet and flushed. "I've my orders, dama." The marshal blinked at his uncomfortable sandals, then looked up hopefully. "But we stopped housebreakers upslope without neglecting duty. I reckon we might do the same with your Clisto." He nodded. "If he's on Navarys, we'll find him."

Mater's smile warmed. "That's all I ask." She looked pointedly at Nikos' hand. The marshal let it fall from Mago's shoulder. She resumed: "Excellent. And I'll take custody of my son. Thank you for fetching him for me!" The dip of her head was as regal as her voice. She placed Mago's hand on her arm and swept him downhill, leaving Nikos behind them.

"Mater, am I to board the caravel with you and Pater?"

Her smile turned saucy. "No." Why was she happy about it?

"I will board the *Subindo* with you!"

Oh. Mago felt a shrinking in his stomach. He'd not welcomed the news of the wave. Who would? But he had anticipated the two weeks free from Mater's supervision . . . buoyantly. And now, he wasn't to have them.

"Our monarch is most gracious," Mater continued. "Such a sympathetic man. He quite saw my point of view."

"But Pater –?"

"You know Zandro won't be parted from his workshop, even if it be packed in crates in the caravel's hold." She sniffed. "Your pater will be –"

"Fine," finished Mago for her.

But Mater fell silent. He turned his head. Evaia below! That was a tear track glistening on her cheek.

"Oh, Mago," she whispered. "I wish he were."

"What's wrong with him?" She'd been about to tell him earlier this afternoon when Phyllos interrupted them. Would she do so now?

"I call it *trull*-disease." She swallowed. "For obvious reasons."

The air grew entirely still, stagnant. Mago had been wrong outside Daymo Ramias' house. That dying of the breeze had been mere precursor, stirred yet by subtle movement. *This* was dead air. He glanced at the sky. A strange yellow tinge darkened the light.

Mago shook his head. Trulls?

He delved through his sense of dread. Why was that term familiar? The view of a cage in the zoological gardens rose in his memory. Three troglodytes – *trulls* – sat behind bars, grooming one another. Mago jerked to a halt.

"No!"

Loathing pulled his voice high and thin. But Mater's label was all too plausible. He'd found that first sight of the trulls disturbing. Monkey-like creatures with long golden fur, they stood hunched and half the heighth of a man. That wasn't the disturbing part. It was their faces, so human, but with – Mago tried to stop there, but his thinking drove onward – with a dumb suffering in their eyes. If Pater's nose elongated and curved just a bit more, it would be a trull nose. And if his ears enlarged, his spine curved – Mago shuddered. "Will he become a trull?"

Mater had stopped with him. Now she drew him forward, restarting their progress down toward the aerodrome. "We don't know." Her reply was matter-of-fact.

"We? Is there a physician who knows about it? Can cure it?" He could hear the eagerness in his questions and bit his lip. *I sound like a little kid.*

"No. Your father and I have discussed it." Mater's haughtiness was creeping back. "Naturally."

"You have to *do* something," Mago insisted.

"Mago, I thought it was time you knew Pater was sick, but your father and I will handle this. You do not have the ordering of our household, and I'll not brook defiance!"

Mago hunched his shoulders, then straightened them. "You wouldn't have told me, if you had a solution in train," he pointed out. Ha! Had he ever stood up to Mater before? It felt good. Really good. Or it would if – Mago sagged again – if they were disputing about something else.

"Mater, do you know why? How did Pater contract this trull-disease? Does someone else have it?"

"It was his research," Mater replied. "And his invention. The new one."

"Making lodestones causes trull-disease?" That couldn't be right.

"Yes. Or no, not exactly."

Mago stifled impatience. His mother relayed social gossip with flawless accuracy, but give her a set of events and she garbled it every time.

"The prototypes, the small lodestones were alright. It was the big one for the ore trams that did it."

"Did what?"

His mother shook her head.

"Mater, what did it do?"

She gripped his hand where it lay on her forearm. "I'm not a fabrimancer, Mago, so I can't really understand it."

Mago tried another question. "What did Pater say?"

"That he'd drawn too much *energea* through his vertices and ripped them from their anchoring. But, Mago, I just don't understand what that means. I can't see the *energea* like Zandro does, nor feel it as you do."

Mago felt his eyes widening. He hadn't known vertices *could* be ripped. None of his lessons on *energea* – theory or practice or protocols – suggested it.

"What *is* a vertex, anyway?" Mater burst out.

"It's where *energea* enters our bodies. There are seven major vertices and fourteen minor ones." How could Mater not know this? Even though she couldn't manipulate the *energea*, it still flowed through her being. And every Navarean learned about it in school, since more had the ability to use it than did not.

"Well, your pater's are drifting from their proper spots." She sounded pettish. "And how to get them back in the right places and anchored, I'm sure I don't know!"

Mago thought that one through. The flow of *energea* between the vertices supported the physical structures of the body. Which meant – Mago was appalled. Moving vertices meant the energy flow was warped, which meant Pater's body was warping to match the deformed *energea*.

That was why Pater's nose and ears were strange.

"Mater . . . this is serious."

She released Mago's arm. "Would I have told you, else?!"

They'd reached the flat streets near the harbor. The aerodrome lay to the north in the fields beyond the city. Not far now. The breeze was picking up again. A sudden gust blew a rubbish bin against the bronze gate of a courtyard, clanging its bars. A storm cloud edged over the peak of Mount Sohlon.

Mater, her lips opening on diatribe, paused, then gripped Mago's arm afresh. "Zandro's condition will wait," she declared. "Hurry! The airships cannot lift into a storm."

Even as she spoke, Mago saw the vast magenta curve of the *Ganador* swell above the roofline of the shops and guild halls. The first of the airships was aloft, rising swiftly at an angle steeper than normal. No doubt the airmen saw the approaching weather too.

❖   ❖   ❖

Liliyah's teeth crunched through pastry, and its honey sweetness spread within her mouth along with the buttery richness of macadamia nuts. Yum! She licked her fingers and looked regretfully at the platter of desserts. *Subindo*'s pantries must be well stocked. Dinner's lavish spread filled her to bursting.

She turned to check on Neoma. The toddler slumped, eyes wrinkled shut, with her chin nodding on the napkin tied beneath it to protect her pinafore. Should Liliyah carry her up to bed?

"Take a break, sweetling," came Eirene's direction from the far end of the table. "I'll need you in the night. Don't spend it all now." Her nurse's gaze was firm and calm. She'd recovered her poise over the meal and looked ready to handle twenty infants, all colicky. A mere sixteen, some too old to be considered babies, would be a piece of cake in comparison.

Except . . . Eirene wouldn't be getting any breaks. Liliyah stood, hoisting little Neoma into her arms. Not so little Neoma – heavy Neoma!

"Liliyah," Eirene's voice chided. "There's plenty of child minding to go round. Let the others have a chance."

Liliyah blinked – what others? – then noticed a boy and two girls from the next table lining up little ones and herding them toward the stairs. She transferred

Neoma to her nurse's waiting arms. Eirene smiled and nudged Liliyah toward the windows. "Sun's setting. Enjoy the sky over the harbor for a bit."

Oh! Caught up in the puppet show earlier, then the bustle of getting young ones down to the dining chamber, and then the savory tastes of her meal, she'd forgotten why she was here, aboard *Subindo*. The beacons at the harbor's outlet, brilliant like evening stars against the green and orange of the horizon, brought it all back. One of the modern caravels, powered by *energea* stones, not sails and wind, passed between the beacons, headed out to sea. Was Mama standing on its deck, gazing at the *Subindo* while Liliyah gazed back? No. Mama's and Papa's caravel would be long gone by now. Good! Far away was safer. But Liliyah felt suddenly alone, despite the hubbub behind her.

She leaned closer to the window, checking for activity on the paving below. The ground crew were busy, transferring the tie-down ropes from the permanent stanchions to the weighted cars that would pull *Subindo* away from the air terminal before the airship launched. Lift would be soon, then.

"Liliyah!" Mago's voice shouted her name. She spun just in time to fend off his embrace. Too many clutching toddler hands and grubby toddler hugs made her resist any more touch. Dama Mytris, over by the stairs with another group of children, raised an eyebrow before turning away. Hadn't Mago said his mother was assigned a sea berth? What was she doing here, supervising youngsters? Surely she'd prefer traveling in luxury, being served, not serving.

"Liliyah!" Mago grabbed her hands, when a side step put her beyond his reaching arms. "Did *you* catch him? Clisto? Did *you* get the lodestones?"

She frowned. "How could I? Mago, I've been busy!"

"When you finished helping Dama Omys, of course."

"But –"

"Liliyah, you knew how important they were. You couldn't have forgotten!" Mago looked stricken. "Did you?" Why did he have to sound forlorn just when she was ready to get angry?

"Mago, I never agreed to help you. I told you: I *trust* Palujon."

Mago revived. "Well you shouldn't! He *is* a thief. I saw him give one of the stones to another aeromancer. So there!"

"So! Maybe his friend is helping him with his project. Didn't you hear him tell your papa that our safety depended on it?"

"Lies to fool Pater. Pater didn't believe him, and neither do I."

Subindo lurched.

Liliyah rocked back on her heels. Mago caught her elbows and steadied her. "Lili, I thought you – I hoped you – I trusted you to have my back!" As he'd held hers just now.

The ground crew was moving the airship away from the terminal, and the breeze was coming in gusts without its shelter. *Subindo* strained at her tethers. The ground crew mounted their stirrups, restraining loops in the ropes that gave the men spots to stand while the airship launched and spools above, within the framework of the dirigible, reeled the ropes and the men in.

Movement away from the focus of activity caught Liliyah's eye. *Azulinike*, emerald green with a silver horse emblazoned on her vast flank, rose into the sky at a steep pitch. Were the airmen worried, that they hurried so? Liliyah craned her neck, trying to see around the bulge of *Subindo* above her. The silk covered framework housing the gas bags blocked the view from the passenger gondola. There it was: *Ganador*, well away, the first of the fleet to embark. And there – ah! the reason for haste – storm clouds boiling up over Mount Sohlon.

"Mago –"

He nodded, his face strained. "Mater and I ran when we saw it. I hope we ran fast enough. They were waiting for me. For us. If the launch goes wrong because of –"

"Because of you searching for those seabound lodestones!" Liliyah burst out, reviving their quarrel.

"Evaia below!" Mago retorted. Except he wasn't responding to her. "It's him!"

Liliyah looked outside again.

Palujon Clisto was racing for the rearmost car. Legs pumping, robes blown by the same gusting wind that Liliyah could feel shuddering the airship, the aeromancer could barely keep his feet. Did he intend to mount *Subindo* via her tethers, as did the ground crew? The men didn't see him. The last one set the brake on the rear car, fitted his foot into a stirrup, and loosed the massive snap hook holding the bouquet of tethers in concert with the men doing the same at the middle and forward cars.

The tethers swung out, released by the snap hook, and rose. Palujon grabbed the one that smacked into his chest, no time to use the stirrup, and wrapped his legs around it.

"Seawrack!" cursed Mago.

Liliyah didn't wait for him, but darted toward the stairs, mercifully empty of children. Up and up and up, she raced, Mago on her heels. Then down the corridor between the staterooms, and through the kitchens where cooks battened down the cabinet doors on sliding soup pots, too harried to notice the intruders.

Bursting out of the sternward door, Liliyah almost paused. The keel passageway was a sort of bridge, running the length of the airship near the bottom of the dirigible framework, but high enough to be uncomfortable. It was narrow, too. Luckily there were hand rails! Liliyah dashed into the cavernous space criss-crossed by immense girders and filled with the first of the enormous saggy gas bags that kept the *Subindo* aloft. She didn't have time to be afraid. Not for herself. Palujon was the one in danger.

The slope of the keelway grew steep as the airship lifted, and its framework thrummed from the buffeting of the wind. Short gangways connected the keelway to stations on the airship's flanks. Engine nacelles? Viewing portholes? Liliyah didn't know or care, but a few held platforms for the tether spools with fabrimancer crew activating the spools. Liliyah ran. Palujon was on one of the rear tethers, the last to be reeled in. The fabrimancers would never get there in time. Would she?

The view from the rear platform was dizzying, despite the modest size of the triangular aperture through the airship's canvas. Rails guarded the platform sides, but the outer edge where the tether rope dangled from its massive spool was open air: no glass, no barrier of any kind. And *Subindo* had climbed high, was headed higher. Liliyah clutched the righthand rail, shrinking from the fall. Navarys lay below, just as it had yesterday, yet not the same. Racing cloud shadows whipped across the island, and an ominous darkness tinged sky and sea. *Subindo*'s framework vibrated and jerked. No pleasure cruise, this.

Liliyah leaned forward. There was Palujon, tiny and tumbled on the end of the rope, snatched by gusting wind. But clinging yet.

Liliyah let go her hold to approach the tether spool.

Mago, arriving abruptly, caromed into her.

She lurched, grabbing something . . . anything . . . nothing. Where was the edge? Had she plunged over it?

"Lili!" Mago screamed.

She felt folds of his clothing in her clutching fingers, felt his grip on her arm, felt . . . firm flooring under her feet. She was safe.

"Hurry!" she gasped, reaching again for the spool.

"Not that way!" corrected Mago. His face was white. "Reach with your vertices, not your fingers."

Of course. They needed to start the *energea* stone controlling the spool, and mere physical touch wouldn't do it.

She re-anchored herself to the railing, closed her eyes, and tried to find calm enough to perform the centering ritual. *Breath in. Breath out.* And . . . *reach* with the *energea* streaming through her right hand. In her mind's perception, a bright note sang out, echoed by a deeper. That was Mago, reaching with her. A trill of notes deeper still answered them. The *energea* stone was awakening. The spool creaked. Had it begun to turn? She peeked through her eyelashes. Yes! The great drum turned over once, then picked up speed. She *reached* harder. Go, go, go! Was Palujon yet attached to the tether's end?

"You do the spool," grunted Mago. "I'll grab Clisto."

"Yes!" She closed her eyes again, poring her concentration into the spinning spool. How long could Palujon hang on? A shout arrowed through the canvas aperture. "Slower!"

Liliyah's stomach clenched. "Evaia, help!" she whispered. And *reached* in a different way, struggling now to brake the massive spool. She'd bet an airship fabrimancer practiced this move many times before taking a ground crewman's life in his hands. At least Palujon *was* attached to that tether. He hadn't fallen.

"Stop!" yelled Mago.

Liliyah's eyes flew open.

She saw Palujon gracefully perched on the small cantilevered step just outside *Subindo*'s canvas, his hand wrapped firmly around the grip at the apex of the opening. The tail end of the rope whipped past his cheek – the spool still revolving much too fast. The aeromancer stepped up to the platform, balanced despite the airship's juddering, stretched out his left hand, and . . . *ohm*! The powerful tone of his *energea* stopped the spool dead.

Liliyah's jaw dropped. How had he done that?

Mago didn't share Liliyah's amazement at Palujon's impressive fabrimancy. Or her relief that everyone was safe. In fact, Mago looked furious, standing with his arms akimbo, his body, tall and stiff.

"Wrack it!" he snarled. "They're not yours! How dare you?"

Palujon lost none of his self possession. Nor was he confused by Mago's unprefaced demand for the lodestones. Liliyah had suffered a moment of "what is he talking about?" when Mago hurled his rebuke.

Palujon stepped past Mago, answering over his shoulder. "My borrowing is, of course, a theft. But I've got five-thousand lives to save, one of them yours! Come on!" He paused a moment beside Liliyah. "Will you help me, demoselle? The fabrimancy will be tricky, and I'll need an assistant."

Liliyah lifted her chin and nodded. *I knew Mago was wrong!* "What must I do?" she asked.

Palujon traversed the short gangway between the platform and the keelway. Liliyah pattered after him. She could hear Mago thumping and puffing behind her. He was still mad, not at all persuaded or mollified by Palujon's sketchy explanation.

The aeromancer strode toward *Subindo*'s stern, instructing while he hastened. "I shall hold back the wind to protect us, but I cannot do that and affix the lodestone to the airship fin, which requires fabrimancy to activate the glue."

Mago pushed past Liliyah to grab Palujon's robes. "I don't care that you claim an errand of mercy." His voice grew pugnacious. "I don't believe you."

The aeromancer kept going despite Mago's hold on him. "Did you not see the storm?" Palujon's light tone held astonishment. "Can you not feel its force?"

The airship shuddered as though a cloud giant had tapped it with his club. Liliyah's grip on the railing kept her on her feet, but Mago went to his knees. Palujon yanked him up, reached his other hand toward Liliyah to grasp her arm, and yelled, "Hold fast!"

If a cloud giant had tapped *Subindo* a moment before, now he batted in earnest. Liliyah felt her feet leave the keelway as the airship plunged, hurled earthward by violent weather. *Subindo*'s frame groaned. Liliyah's hold on the railing broke. Evaia below! Where would a tumble through the vast girder-threaded interior land her?

But Palujon's grip remained fast, and three descending chords – more fabrimancy at work – held him on the keelway, both children anchored there with him. *Subindo*'s dive ended as abruptly as it began, and Liliyah's legs trembled under the sudden press of the metal beneath her feet.

"This is no ordinary tempest." Palujon started for the stern as soon as he saw Liliyah and Mago were steady again. "Just as Evaia shrugs and the seabed moves, so does her sister Caecia spin, and the airs swirl. This is the great wind, the *typhon*, and these love pats, a mere prelude. I must attach two lodestones to *Subindo*'s tail fins, else she perishes in the maelstrom."

Mago's face, glancing back at Liliyah, whitened. Now did he believe? His lips moved – "no" – but his eyes – horror in their depths – said "yes."

The keelway ended at a metal ladder climbing a vertical girder, one of nearly thirty radiating out from a central spoke to the perimeter of *Subindo*'s frame. Surrounding rings attached at each rung gave some protection to a climber, but Liliyah's belly shivered as she ducked inside the first when Palujon beckoned. The ladder vibrated as Mago and then Palujon hustled after her.

The platform at the top, on the level with the airship's central spoke, stretched wide enough for two triangular apertures, one to each side of the *Subindo*'s vertical rudder fin, accessing the top surfaces of the horizontal elevator fins. *Subindo* had risen into the clouds, and scurrying mists fled across Liliyah's view. She shrank against the hand rail – Evaia be thanked there were hand rails! – flinching as *Subindo* moaned. Mago joined her; then Palujon arrived in a flurry of melody. Was that why the openings in the airship's canvas funneled no wind inside to the platform? Palujon wielded his *energea* even now to protect them? He seemed to require no railing to keep his balance.

"Mago, are you willing to help?" Palujon asked. "*Subindo*'s girth dwarfs those of her sister ships. Placing both lodestones together, rather than sequentially, is safest, but I'll not constrain you."

Mago's throat worked soundlessly.

"Quickly, now. Yes or no?"

"Yes," Mago croaked.

"Good. Listen." And Palujon issued his instructions. Within his bubble of still air, Liliyah and Mago would each advance onto an elevator fin and place their lodestones against the vertical fin, using the rearmost hoof of the unicorn painted on the sheathing as a target. On the aeromancer's count, they would use *energea* to activate the glue adhering to each lodestone. "You must keep your balance," he enjoined. "I will still the wind, and I can steady you, but some effort you must make of your own."

Liliyah nodded, gulping. Her head for heights was normally good, but surely this demanded something more. Palujon's melody slowed and deepened. The cloud wisps traveling over *Subindo*'s fins lost speed and drifted, even while those outside the aeromancer's restraint blew faster.

"Go now." Palujon's bidding was quiet.

Liliyah bent to fit through the opening in the canvas . . . and didn't arise once outside. *Seawrack!* She'd never ever imagined herself standing on an airship's tail fin – its metallic surface humming amidst the violence of a hurricane. This was crazy! She crouched lower, heart pounding.

There was reason for confidence. Palujon's still air surrounded her, protecting her from the buffet of the storm. The elevator fin under her feet spread wide, wider than the parlor back home, although not as deep. If she flung herself forward, lying flat, her fingertips wouldn't quite reach the edge. But, oh! This was no place of comfort.

She sidled closer to the vertical rudder fin. Its metallic skin felt cold to her touch, cold and smooth. She couldn't grip it like a railing, but its looming solidity eased the racing chaos of cloud and wind. She inched closer to the unicorn's rear hoof. If only the beast faced to the rear instead of forward. Then she wouldn't have get so near to the drop. The elevator fin notched in there, presenting a nasty abyss of roiling mist.

Subindo jerked downward as the wind outside Palujon's control gusted and howled.

Liliyah curled, seeking a solid surface even as the fin bounced under her. *Goddess!* She came to rest right beneath the unicorn's hoof, much too close to the v-notch.

"You're there," came Palujon's calm voice. "Reach up."

She reached. *Wrack it!* Nowhere close enough to that hoof. She would have to get her feet under her and stand. It seemed impossible.

"Don't think. Just do it," Palujon urged.

Don't think, straighten up, she urged herself. Her legs felt cold and stiff, but she rearranged her feet sole down. *Now*. And pushed herself straight. Well, straighter. Could she reach the hoof now? Almost.

"Good!" Palujon approved. "Open your *energea* sense."

No difficulty there. Palujon's notes had sung to her all through her ordeal. Her ear for the *energea* was open. She *reached* to perceive Mago's lodestone on the other side of the rudder fin, to hear its faint song. Was it in place? Where? Where? Ah! There! Just a touch . . . rearward. Liliyah heard a whimper escape her lips. She would have to shift closer to that dreadful drop.

Then *Subindo* dropped and juddered again.

Stretching to reach over her head, not crouched like last time, Liliyah fought for balance, swaying left, then right, the abyss looming. No! She slung herself forward against the rudder fin and stuck, somehow, sheer will acting as glue. She flung her right hand up, lodestone clenched in her fingers, and *reached*. An arpeggio of sparkling notes shimmered. The adhesive on the lodestone melted, then hardened. She'd done it! Evaia below! She barely noticed her scramble back through the aperture to safety.

Mago tumbled onto the platform an instant later, grinning and manic. "We did it, we did it, we did it! Sea's bells!" he chanted. And grabbed her into his frantic arms, pressing his brow to hers. "Are you alright?"

She'd heard the true note of his *energea* – clear, neither sharp nor flat – as he placed his lodestone exactly right. So odd to realize that, as a kinesthetic fabrimancer, he *felt* the *energea* rather than hearing it. But he was right. They'd done it. She turned her head for Palujon's confirmation.

And didn't get it.

The aeromancer posed on the platform like a charioteer, legs straddled, arms extended to control invisible reins of *energea*, focused on completing his task, every bit as demanding as theirs had been. His energetic music swelled loud and louder, powerful notes, vigorous and fast. The crescendo peaked, hit a cymbal crash, then silenced. And *Subindo*'s juddering ceased, transitioning abruptly to the quiet of smooth sailing. Liliyah's breath huffed out.

And Palujon opened his eyes.

"*Subindo* is stable and will remain unharmed by wind so long as those lodestones stay in place to channel the air. Mago, you can remove them and return them to your father when you dock in Imsterfeldt. *Energea* will release the adhesive."

Mago's arms fell from Liliyah's shoulders, and he turned to face the aeromancer. "I –, I –," he stammered.

The "I told you so!" that would have burst from Liliyah in other circumstances, didn't. She could only grin, happy Palujon had justified her faith in him, happier still that they were safe.

"I should have known," Mago blurted. "I did know! I just –"

"Trusted your father," finished Palujon. "Of course you did. Why shouldn't you?"

Mago's face acquired a stern expression. "Because – because he'd given me reason to doubt him, that's why." Good for Mago. Loyalty kept him from criticizing his pater to a stranger, but didn't keep him from owning he'd been wrong. "And I'm sorry. If I'd gotten those lodestones back from you . . ."

Liliyah shuddered. If Palujon hadn't stolen those lodestones, *Subindo* would be hurtling earthward, seaward, to be broken on the waves. Waves? *Evaia below*! *The* wave! Liliyah peered through the stern aperture again. The airship was climbing, tilting her bow upward, yielding a better view over her tail fins. She broke from the cloud occupying that stretch of sky to emerge under the greater cloud cover spreading above. Navarys lay at some distance, on the horizon, hurrying gray sky wrack above its mountain, pewter gray sea surging around its coastline. The tiny dots of the caravels speckled the ocean below *Subindo*, most well away from the dangerous shallows ringing the island. But not all. Liliyah could just discern two yet at anchor in the harbor, one sailing between the beacons at its outlet.

Mago hissed. What was he noticing?

Then she saw it too: a strange swelling or bulging of the salt deeps below. As she watched, a prominence formed, a ridge gaining height as it raced toward toward Navarys. "No," she whispered, and felt Mago's hand take hers. "Oh, no."

At the last, she couldn't look, couldn't bear to witness the wave lunging down on the straggling caravels, breaking over the city, foaming up the slopes of Mount Sohlon. A sob escaped Mago, and she opened her eyes. He did not weep, despite the sob, but his eyes were stricken.

"I must go," Palujon announced softly. He was securing the lodestone wallet in his belt pouch, strapping it closed, checking its buckles.

What?

"The *Belezea* and the *Magnifikat* need me."

"But how? And there's only one lodestone left!" exclaimed Mago.

"One will suffice. Provided I hasten."

"You can't!" Liliyah felt her heart thumping. "You mustn't! It's too late. They've sailed! And if they hadn't – Still it would be too late!"

Palujon smiled gently. "My aeromancy will get me to *Belezea*. I can sense her in the storm. Finding *Magnifikat* will be harder, stabilizing her, harder still. But, I *am* an aeromancer!"

"No!" Liliyah barely knew why she protested. Except she did. Palujon's words made his task sound easy. But it would not be easy, no. Desperate and dangerous and chancy. "Please!"

"Lili –" Palujon's voice grew firm. "The children on those two airships deserve life too."

She gasped and nodded.

"Be well." It was all happening too fast. His parting came even as he sprang through the aperture, sprinted across the tail fin, and leaped into the air amidst a shower of *energea* notes, limbs spread as though they were wings. And perhaps they were, for he did not fall, soaring outward and up, a scrap of silhouette in the vast gray of the sky, headed straight for the cloud fragment *Subindo* had just exited.

Liliyah burst into tears.

"Ssh, ssh." Mago's arms were around her again, enfolding her, comforting her. But she was not comforted. Palujon's goodbye had been so final.

Two weeks later, *Subindo* sailed into Imsterfeldt's skies. The day was bright and breezy, sunshine bringing vividness and cheer to the scene below. Liliyah stared eagerly at the tall stone houses, packed tightly shoulder to shoulder, and the many canals angling inland from the harbor. Coolness flowed through the airship's partially open casements along with the fishy scent of the wharves and faint applause from the crowd in the central square. So *this* was the mighty trading port of the continent. This was . . . home?

She glanced aside to Mago. His shoulder felt warm and solid against hers. He smiled. "We're here."

So they were, all thousand and some of them. The divans of *Subindo*'s sitting area overflowed with eight- and nine-year-olds, murmuring, poking one another, or gawking out the windows. A few older girls exchanged glances – should we restrain the unruly ones? – then shrugged and ignored the racket. The younger tots and their nurses filled the dining rooms on the level above. No one wanted to be shut away in the windowless staterooms.

The voyage had been grueling. The pantries ran low after a week's worth of tempting meals; the tureens of porridge, rice, and beans that followed grew repulsive quickly. Infants wailed, toddlers cried for their mamas, the school children played pranks or were sick or whined they were bored. And Liliyah's attempts to amuse Eirene's bunch failed more often than not after the first few days.

The storm, with its driving rain and powerful winds, affected *Subindo* not at all. She sailed serenely through the tempest. Whatever Palujon had done worked. The airship's captain and crew marveled, even as they performed the tasks normal to sailing: trimming the vessel, monitoring altitude, charting their progress. They knew, of course, about the lodestones. When Liliyah and Mago descended from the rear platform, two grim-faced sailors escorted them to the bridge where Captain Balthazar demanded explanations. And allowed himself to be mollified by what he heard. He even went so far as to offer them a complete tour of the working areas of the airship, as well as a turn manning the helm.

The storm blew itself out in three days. Liliyah found herself retreating to the crew areas whenever

Eirene sent her on break. Where else could she get away from all the whiny, naughty brats infesting *Subindo*? And the crewmen welcomed her, feting her as the heroine who helped save their ship.

But now her ordeal was over. They'd be disembarking soon.

Mago nudged her. "Look," he said. "The mooring tower."

Subindo had passed over Imsterfeldt to the marshlands beyond. A series of dikes created dry meadows where cows grazed the grasses surrounding the tower. Three more towers receded in the distance. The nearer flew the magenta-striped bulk of – "*Ganador*!" exclaimed Liliyah, while Mago murmured, "*Azulinike*!" The emerald green airship, anchored at the far tower, showed damage from her passage through the hurricane, her rudder hanging askew and one elevator fin torn away entirely. Nor had *Ganador* emerged unscathed, Liliyah noted. A long gash in her canvas marred one flank, with the ragged end of a broken girder protruding. Was Palujon that much more skilled than the aeromancers who protected the damaged pair? Or was one lodestone each insufficient?

Subindo's nose cone glided closer to the mooring tower. Liliyah held her breath. The maneuver seemed tricky: the airship so large, the tower unyielding. Then the fore tether shot across the gap to be secured by ground crew. *Subindo* came gently to a halt. Sudden pandemonium erupted within the sitting area.

Liliyah found herself jumping up and down at the bow exit, holding Mago's hand while the mob of excited kids jostled behind them. The door swung open, and she darted across the gangway, feeling its metal vibrating under her thumping feet, then the solid flagging of the tower balcony. And, oh!

"Papa! Mama! Papa!" They were here. They were both here. Safe and sound and *here*! She tumbled into her father's arms.

Liliyah smiled and lifted her pen. That reunion still lived in her memory, a confusion of joy and sadness, relief and anticipation. With reason. Her old life on Navarys had ended, her new one in Imsterfeldt, just begun in Papa's embrace.

A gull cried outside, its strident voice loud through the open casement over her desk. She looked up from her parchment, sniffing the seawrack on the air, surveying the pointed roofscape of Imsterfeldt beyond the dry meadows surrounding her tower. *Subindo*, a more faded blue than she'd been two decades ago, approached the tower nearest the city, preparing for dock. The two towers between the airship and Liliyah's home stood decrepit and abandoned, crumbling a little more with each winter's onslaught.

Once word of *Belezea*'s crash in far Bazinthiad came north, the fourth tower – now Liliyah's home – was auctioned off to the highest bidder: Daymo Lykos, as it chanced. Three mooring stations provided adequate space for three airships and the remote chance of lost *Magnifkat* turning up. Then *Ganador* and *Azulinike* were retired after a mere five years of flight, too battered from their passage through the storm to stay air-worthy without the sophisticated repair facilities of Navarys.

Liliyah studied the ink drying on the scroll before her.

Was she right to get the story down so? The true story? She and Mago had argued about it. Mago, still remorseful from misjudging Palujon, wanted to proclaim him a hero, see him honored on gala days, and his name given to public buildings. Liliyah was not so sure.

"He cared for what he did, not for what people thought." Palujon's indifference to Mago's scorn and disdain arose so definitively in her memory. *I know I'm right about that*. "And he did what he set out to do: save the lives of all on *Ganador*, *Azulinike*, and *Subindo*."

"He deserves our remembrance."

"He has mine. Yours."

"Everyone's!" Mago was stubborn.

Then the last caravel docked at Imsterfeldt's quays – the derelict, surviving the wave against all expectation – and bringing news of lost ships. Zandro Mytris had drowned under the wave on one of them.

Pomp and and an outpouring of grief accompanied his funeral, attended by nearly all the Navarean exiles, as well as their monarch (who'd been hustled to safety against his will by friends). Daymo Mytris had been a popular and renowned figure. Mago held his tongue for his mater's sake, but chafed under his private knowledge. Had his pater prevailed, the funeral services would have commemorated the deaths of five thousand children. As it was . . .

When word of *Belezea*'s crash came north, Mago reopened their disagreement.

"The airship's a wreck of twisted girders, but every last passenger on *Belezea* survived the landing accident. Because of Palujon. *Palujon!*" Mago glared. "It's not right! We have the Zandro Mytris Academy of Fabrimancy, but the only mention of Palujon Clisto is as a rogue who tried to steal the lodestones that saved us."

"But Palujon is dead."

"We don't know what happened to *Magnifikat*. And we do know that he made it away from *Belezea*. Just like he soared away from *Subindo*."

"But he's not *here*, Mago. And Ione *is*. Palujon would rather history marked him a thief than destroy your mother's happiness. She clings to your father's heroism. It's all she has left, now that he's gone."

"Clisto's already reviled," Mago grumbled, "doomed to go down in ignominy."

And it seemed he was right. Palujon's reputation had not changed for the better since Mago uttered those words. She glanced at her manuscript again. *I'm setting the record straight at last.*

Giggles on the stairs recalled Liliyah to the present.

"Is she there? Is she?" came the laughing voice of her daughter.

"Nah, Papa said she's pulling horsetail stalks out of the butterwort." That was her son, up to mischief, from the signs of it. "We'll sneak in, check behind the hangings and in the study nook, and then pull the casket out from the under the desk."

"But it's locked!" Did little Ismene sound shocked. "Mama keeps it locked."

"Pooh! My fabrimancy's up to that! I'll have it open in a trice," boasted Ismene's brother.

Liliyah swiveled, turning her back to the desk. Two tangled, curly heads popped above the tread of the last step, followed by the shoulders, torsos, and feet of her children. They stopped, appalled to see their mother, very much present in this chamber and not five floors down in the garden.

"Oh!"

"Mama!"

"So you've become a lock picker with your fabrimancy, eh?" Liliyah questioned her son.

"Er . . ."

She'd kept her tone light, but he knew he'd no business nosing through her things. Especially not *those* things. For the lodestones had proved less safe than her papa had asserted, back in the Navarean exhibition hall. It seemed that proper *energea* stones exerted some protective effect that was lacking for a practitioner using a lodestone or acting without a stone altogether. And that was a serious problem. Daymo Mytris was the first to catch the trull-disease, but unfortunately not the last.

When a fabrimancer pulled immense flows of *energea* in his or her working, a traditional stone channeled the better part of the power through its vertices. The lodestones divided the current strictly in half, and if that half were too much for the fabrimancer's vertices, he or she developed the trull symptoms. Liliyah shook her head. Imsterfeldt's physicians were working on a cure. And they needed one. There weren't enough *energea* stones to go around to all the new students of fabrimancy. No deposits of the star-stone needed to make them had yet been discovered on the continent. And practicing fabrimancy with neither *energea* stone nor lodestone was even more risky.

"The sanctum of a thaumaturge is no place for prying," she chided her son.

"Ho! *I'm* a thaumaturge," he bragged.

His sister nudged him. More prudent, perhaps?

"Are you now?" Liliyah injected amusement into her words. "What was your father telling me just last night? Something about your desk at the academy belching green phosphor?"

"Aw! Mama!"

"Liliyah? Is Alex with you?" Mago's deep voice rumbled from the floor below. The tromp of her husband's feet on the stair treads followed the called question. "His bedchamber's knee deep in mess, and I told him he needn't beg my permission to attend the mummer's play with his friends until the chamber was tidy."

Alex squirmed, and Ismene's eyes widened.

"Ah, ha!" Mago arrived, taking the last few steps in a bound. "Pestering your mother, are you?" Well, it was more serious than that. She and Mago would need to discuss more secure storage for the lodestones. But an end to this interruption by her progeny, so she could finish her record of Palujon's deeds, would be nice. "Come away, culprits!" Mago sang out, passing around the children to touch Liliyah's hand and brush her cheek with a kiss. "Another turn of the glass?" he inquired.

"Less than that. A half turning should suffice."

Mago's left brow twitched up. He knew her too well. Half a turning became three all too easily, when she grew absorbed enough. "Alright, one then," she corrected herself.

Mago nodded, grinned, and shepherded their son and daughter downstairs.

Liliyah indulged reverie for a moment. Alex and Ismene were so precious, despite their occasional naughtiness. Might a third child come to her? She and Mago both hoped for it. Eirene was getting a bit old to help with an infant, but even she had expressed a wish for another small Mytris in the nursery.

Liliyah swiveled back around to face her desk.

Should she complete her story of how Palujon saved the children of Navarys? Or would burning the scroll be the better choice?

She dipped her quill in the ink pot, wrote three more paragraphs, and then a last one.

If, perhaps, you find this scroll in an odd cranny among the bones of the ancient world, then you'll know I spared it from the flames. And you'll know that Palujon Clisto was no rogue.

There. It was done. For well or ill, done.

She sprinkled sand on the trailing curve of the parchment, shook it clean, and rolled it closed. What now?

Liliyah *reached*, hearing the merry music of her *energea* gilding the scroll with . . . blessing.

THE END

Timeline for the North-lands Stories

ANCIENT TIMES

Skies of Navarys..................3000 years before *Troll-magic*

THE BRONZE AGE

Resonant Bronze ....2000 years before *Troll-magic*

BEFORE THE STEAM AGE

Rainbow's Lodestone.......... ~100 years before *Troll-magic*

Star-drake........... immediately after *Rainbow's Lodestone*

THE STEAM AGE

Sarvet's Wanderyar ....52 years before *Troll-magic*

Crossing the Naiad .. concurrent with *Sarvet's Wanderyar*

Livli's Gift ....38 years after *Sarvet's Wanderyar*
(14 years before *Troll-magic*)

Troll-magic ....the now of this timeline

The Troll's Belt .... contemporaneous with *Troll-magic*

Perilous Chance .... contemporaneous with *Troll-magic*

J.M. Ney-Grimm lives with her husband and children in Virginia, just east of the Blue Ridge Mountains. She's learning about permaculture gardening, post-carbon preparation, and debunking popular myths about food. The rest of the time she reads Robin McKinley and Lois McMaster Bujold, plays boardgames like Settlers of Catan, *rears her twins, and writes stories set in her troll-infested North-lands.*

Look for her novels and novellas at your favorite bookstore – online or on Main Street.

J.M. Ney-Grimm maintains a blog featuring flash fiction from her North-lands and other tidbits unearthed by her ever-active curiosity.

Visit her at JMNey-Grimm.com.